A Valley of Shadow

A Tale of Izrak the Deathless

Lee Patton

The Arcanist: Fantasy Publishing

The Arcanist: Fantasy Publishing, LLC

Bloomington, Indiana, United States.

Websites: thearcanist.net | magazine.thearcanist.net

Contact: business@thearcanist.net

Support: support@thearcanist.net

First serialized online: February 2025

First paperback/hardcover editions: October 2025

First ebook edition: October 2025

Paperback ISBN: 979-8-9923135-5-0
Hardcover ISBN: 979-8-9923135-6-7
eBook ISBN: 979-8-9923135-7-4

For Anastasia, my love,

who taught me that fantasy is anything but…

Acknowledgement

A special thank you to James D. Mills, for his ruthless encouragement and undying support, and for his tireless efforts to share the dreams of others.

Dreaming, he stands upon the shores of dusk,

As the dark waters course beneath his soles,

No longer whole, withered, an empty husk

Among the old and desiccated boles.

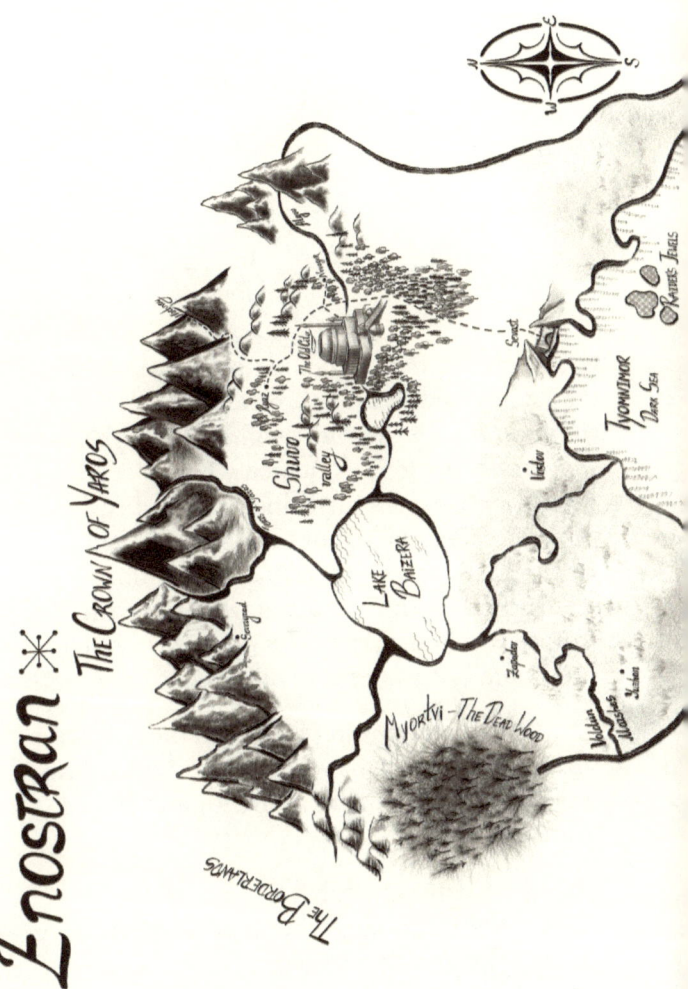

Enostran ✳ The Crown of Yaros

The Borderlands

Myortvi – The Dead Wood

Lake Bnizeria

Shuvo Valley

Tyovnimor Dark Sea

Knife Jags

PRELUDE

EVEN THE DEAD SUFFER

Lord Yemor slumped onto a log the villains had conceived to use as a bench. *Peasants. How is it that these sorts never consider stealing decent furniture?* The lord wondered what price he would now pay for anything bearing a cushion. A grimace parted Yemor's lips as he looked at the dead man sitting across from him. He had not even considered what price the corpse would demand. *This undead churl will undoubtedly try to ransom me himself.*

"They were waiting for us." Yemor drank from a half-empty wineskin, then sighed. "Tell me, Izrak Laav. Is there a cure for a wretched soul?"

Seated on a crate, Izrak hunched over his longsword, running a whetstone along its edges. The grinding ceased. The dead man peered over the crackling tongues of flame at Yemor. The shadows of his hollowed eyes flickered with the firelight, his lipless grin broad between his desiccated, pallid cheeks.

"Only one that I know of," the dead man said, voice the rasp of wind over an endless sea of sand.

The lord stared at that spectral visage, leaned back and, after a moment, looked away. *As if Varon's cells were not torturous enough.* This hideous creature was more than Yemor's delicate sensibilities could withstand. *I'm going to flay whoever hired this monster to rescue me.* He waved his hand, laughed.

"That's what I appreciate about you warriors of the Call. Great sense of humor. Always smiling." He chuckled and took another pull of the wine.

Izrak lowered his gaze, resumed sharpening his blade.

Yemor held the wineskin upside-down in front of him, lips pinched, eyes squinting. He shook it. *Empty.* He sighed, tossed the skin to the ground and rose from his seat. The lord stretched his back as he surveyed the carnage on display in the glade. A dozen bodies littered the camp, hewn and maimed. The faces of the brigands were flaxen beneath the full moon, contorted in a fear born not entirely of the wounds they suffered, terrible though they were.

"Did you truly have to do all that?" The lord's arm swept over the scene in a grandiose gesture.

"You did tell those wretched souls to run."

Yemor bent with laughter.

Izrak stowed the whetstone and stood, sliding his sword into its scabbard. "It is time. Those who had the sense to flee will return with more men. We must reach the Myortvi before then." The dull glint on the iron studs of his leather jerkin faded away as he stamped out the fire.

* * *

"Keep low and stay behind me," Izrak said. "The moon's light will be of no help once we are inside."

Yemor trailed him at a cautious distance as they approached the edge of the Myortvi. "Light a torch, then."

The foolish lord did not understand. *The living never can.* The Myortvi—The Dead Woods—was more than some forsaken forest in the borderlands of Enostran. It was a place of evil, of shadow. Ageless and unchanging, the dead wood gave nothing but only took from those who would travel its tortured paths, piece by piece, until nothing remained. Izrak's journeys carried him through the dark wood with relative frequency, and the mercenary would often wonder, as he trudged beneath its abyssal canopy, if he should not simply remain. In the end, what more could the dead wood take? Was that place not fitting for one such as him? Countless arcane horrors prowled that realm of perpetual dusk, and none suffered the light to pass within its fetid reaches. *Why did she send us this way?* Any sign of life would be consumed.

"No fire."

"Then how are we supposed to see, Izrak? We'll be lost for sure." Yemor stopped, placed his pudgy hands on his hips. "Well?"

Izrak continued a few paces, then halted. Standing deathly still, he faced away from the lord as his fingers closed around a frayed pouch on his belt. *Lost … For over three centuries, you have held me in your grasp. Why will you not show me the way? Why do you keep me blind?* After a moment, he shifted his dead gaze upon the quivering lord. The mercenary's eyes were black pits, features ephemeral in the silver light of the moon.

"The darkness holds no secrets from me."

Lord Yemor quickened his pace, shuffling behind the mercenary as he moved on. "Easy for you … What does a corpse have to fear?"

"I fear many things."

Yemor snorted. "But how could you be afraid? You're already dead."

Izrak stopped before a mangled tree at the wood's edge, warped, twisted beyond recognition, its blackened bark peeling away in curling strips. *Just like me.* He ran his pale, skeletal fingers over the shriveled bark. "Even the dead can suffer." A flutter of wings drew his attention skyward; a murder of crows, concealed within night's black shroud, flitted by overhead from the direction of the brigand's campsite, their midnight meal disturbed by unwelcome intruders. *Perhaps I have lingered here for too long …* A hollow sigh passed from the mercenary as he drew his sword, its nicked, razor edges gleaming in the moonlight. "Come, my lord. Varon's men will not be far behind."

"Must we go through these wretched woods? Surely there must be another way." Yemor retreated a step, staring at the gnarled, barren branches reaching into the night— fingers of the damned clawing out of some ancient hell.

The mercenary glanced left, then right. "There are. Three of them." Izrak adjusted his worn leather skullcap. "We can go around, two leagues to the north, three to the south. Or we could make it easy for Varon and simply go back."

Trembling beneath his thick, sable furs, Lord Yemor peered back down the serpentine path. He breathed in deep, released it. "The woods, then."

"So be it. Hold onto my belt. Do not let go."

Yemor reached a shaking, hesitant hand toward the mercenary.

Izrak grunted. "Fear not. There are worse terrors in these woods than I."

A screeching howl pierced the dread silence of the night. Answering calls echoed throughout the dark wood.

"What was that?" Yemor said, grasping the mercenary's belt.

Izrak looked over his shoulder, his maw drawn in its eternal grin of rotted, yellow teeth. "Guuls."

* * *

The darkness was suffocating. Although, it may simply have been the rancid stench of the corpse shambling ahead as the lord trailed behind. All around, branches rattled in the fell wind, twigs snapped, and owls sang in unseen congregation—a solemn dirge for the passing of two lost souls. Yemor pinched the bridge of his nose, finger and thumb coming away slick with sweat. *How can he see in this?* A dull pain throbbed at the backs of his eyes, the strain of peering into the preternatural black of the woods plaguing the lord with a headache. *How much longer must I suffer this place? This corpse?*

"Are we almost out?"

"Quiet," the dead man said. His frame went rigid beneath his jerkin and mail coat. He stopped.

The lord stumbled into him, like walking into a stone wall. Yemor grunted. "What is it?"

Izrak gave no reply.

Useless though it was, Yemor flicked his gaze from side to side. He scowled, furrowed his brow. The owls' song had fallen away. The winds ceased, the woods, still. His skin broke out with gooseflesh. Suddenly, a scratching— claws dragging over wood—tore through the silence. Shivering, the lord snapped his head in the direction of the horrid sound. A branch cracked. Yemor yelped, slapped a hand over his mouth.

A keening wail shattered the turgid air. Rapid footfalls charged in from the right, the attendant wail growing louder. Yemor flinched as the noise drew closer. The air whistled on the edge of a blade—the wail cut off in an instant.

Foul blood spattered over the lord's cheek. His nails bit into bloodless palms as his grip tightened on the dead man's belt.

The Myortvi erupted in a storm of ripping claws and ravenous cries. "Run." Izrak took off.

Stumbling after the mercenary, clinging desperately to his belt, Yemor's stout legs struggled in a terrified frenzy to keep pace. Horror closed in on all sides as clicking fangs and blood-curdling shrieks haunted each step. But every time the monsters came near, they were consumed by the whip and whistle of Izrak's sword as it sang its song of death.

And yet, the number of the wretched guuls seemed to increase. Sweat, now mixed with blood, poured over Yemor's brow, his ragged breaths coming in wheezing gasps. The dead man stopped, and the lord crashed into him. Yemor's stiff fingers slipped from Izrak's belt as he was sent sprawling across the ground.

"Damn you, hell-spawn." Heart hammering in his chest, he threw out his hands in a flailing attempt to retake hold of his macabre guardian. Yemor's fingers found cold flesh. "Izrak?"

Claws gripped the lord's shoulders, pinning him to the ground as a hot breath washed over his face in rank waves. Yemor shriveled and

whimpered, a feral snarl the only reply. The
creature's obscured face hung over his own.
Yemor's fingers sank into the cold mud as
jagged fangs brushed against his neck.

"Izrak …" he said, throat choked with fear
and disgust. *That monster abandoned me, left me
to die.* "Help me!"

A whistling slice fell from above, ending
in a dull smack of steel on flesh. The snarling
ended in a whine. Hot blood sprayed the lord's
face as the monster's body slumped against his,
then rolled away.

A hand closed around the collar of Yemor's
tunic, pulling the lord to his feet in one fluid
motion. "On your … feet," the dead man
rasped.

Yemor ran a hand over his face, wiping
away the blood, his body quaking as his mouth
opened and closed wordlessly.

"Need to … run …"

"Just get me out of here!" The lord felt
Izrak's hand tighten on his collar before pulling
him closer. The dead man's hand trembled.
Yemor's skin crawled. He heard the grinding
clatter of teeth just above his head. His
stomach twisted as the lord tried to back away,
but the dead man held him fast. "Unhand me,
corpse." Frigid fingers closed around his throat.

Branches split as a mass of screeching fury collided with the dead man. Yemor heard the hollow thud of Izrak's sword hitting the mud as his hand was torn away from the lord's throat. "Izrak!" Yemor staggered back, hearing claws rake over chainmail amid the guuls' wails and snapping jaws. He turned, about to run, when a very human roar exploded from the shadows. The lord froze as terror turned his blood to ice.

The bloody squelch of tearing flesh and the ripping crack of breaking bones assailed the lord's senses. *Just get me out of here …* The howling of the guuls turned to fearful whines before being stifled one by one. *Don't let them take me …* Yemor closed his eyes, hearing teeth sinking into meat as he covered his ears. *Not like this …*

After a time, Yemor opened his eyes and held his hands out in front of him. All was quiet in the dead wood once more. The lord stumbled forward a step. "Izrak? Are you there? What the hell happened to you?"

A pair of yellow orbs, dim embers smoldering in the shadows, materialized several paces away. Mud squelched beneath heavy boots as the orbs rose slowly to the height of a tall man. The embers burned out. Disembodied steps approached the lord. Yemor heard the rattle of mail, then the clack of a sword falling into its scabbard. A fell presence lingered in front of him, its dead chill prickling his flesh.

"Come, my lord. We are near the end." Izrak's rasp seethed from the black.

"What about the guuls?" Yemor said. "Surely there are more of them. We won't make it."

"They will trouble us no longer."

"How do you know?"

"They are afraid."

* * *

Flickering torchlight and the nervous chatter of Lord Yemor's retinue greeted them as Izrak led the nobleman out of the Myortvi. A carriage sat on the rough trail, surrounded by two dozen mounted men-at-arms. As the mercenary and his charge approached, a figure emerged from the carriage, hooded and cloaked in black. *Always with me.* The mercenary's pace slowed, fingers closing around his age-worn pouch.

"So, it was you who hired this corpse to rescue me." Yemor strode forward as Izrak stopped a few paces away. "Lady Olesia."

At this, the lady lowered her hood. Olesia's raven hair shimmered in the firelight, bound at the crown with a silver circlet, a rich amethyst at its center glittering upon her porcelain brow. Her ashen eyes were storms, roiling clouds streaked with flecks of violet lightning. The corners of her mauve lips curled upward as she closed her eyes and bowed.

Lord Yemor chuckled. "And what was the promised payment?"

Lady Olesia leaned in, whispered in his ear.

The lord snorted. "Is that all?" Yemor laughed as he moved past Olesia towards the carriage. "Very well." He climbed inside. "And to think, I would've given him a castle, but I suppose a tomb is more fitting for a corpse." The lord sneered, slamming the carriage door shut.

Izrak held Olesia's gaze as she stepped closer to him. The lady stared into the empty pits of his eyes, a smile creeping onto her lips. *What does she see there?* A moment passed. The lady drew a tattered, browned scroll from the folds of her sleeve and held it out to him.

Izrak took the scroll. "The location. It is inside?"

The lady nodded, then held out a small leather purse. Izrak tilted his head. Olesia stepped forward, took his hand, and placed the purse on his palm. The mercenary stared into Olesia's eyes as his fingers closed around it. "Thank you." Her hand held his for a heartbeat, for two. She let go.

Olesia pulled her hood over her head and turned away. She climbed into the carriage, and the lord's retinue departed. Several of the men-at-arms cast glances back at the mercenary as they rode along the trail.

Izrak watched for a time as the cavalcade faded into the gloom on the horizon. *Olesia …* The moon hung low over the foothills rolling in the west, its pale light giving way to the crimson of encroaching dawn. *In another time, perhaps …* His fingers played along the woven surface of the pouch at his hip, the Record of Kosh clutched in the other hand. *At last, I will find you.* The mercenary placed the scroll in his satchel. He turned and trudged along the Myortvi towards the jagged peaks rising in the north, the Crown of Yaros. *And my suffering will finally come to an end.*

PROLOGUE

No one expects a dead man to walk through the front door. This time was no different. The dozen patrons of the Soul's Lament went silent as the cobbled door whined on its hinges, and Izrak Laav crossed over the threshold, ducking his head as he passed inside.

A trio of men, grim faces flushed, eyes glazed in a half-drunken stupor, sat at a table near the door. Shifting in their chairs as the dead man approached, they whispered as quivering hands hovered over unseen knives. Izrak glanced at the vagrants, the iron studs of his jerkin and mail coat glinting in the flickering torchlight. They withered under the glare of eyeless pits and yellowed gleam of his lipless grin.

The dead man moved on, his pale hand falling away from the pommel of his longsword.

Izrak took a seat at what had become his customary table, in a dark corner at the far end of the tavern. Unhooking his scabbard from his belt, he placed the sword against the moldering wall beside him. Resting his mail-coated elbows on the table, Izrak leaned over, ran his fingertips through the few strands of blonde hair hanging from under his worn-leather skullcap. Of course, whatever soothing sensation this used to bring was now illusory. The dead man could not feel it. Old habits...

Rats scurried across the swollen, rotten floorboards, their scratching blending with the torrents of rain cascading over the walls outside. The incessant drone grew louder the more he sought to block it out.

"Izrak Laav, dread mercenary and favored customer!" A sonorous voice sounded from behind the bar counter. "What can I provide for Nochnoy's most intransigent soul?"

"You missed your calling as a poet," Izrak said, his voice a rasp of wind over an endless sea of sand. "The usual, Evpat."

A snicker cut through the din. "The usual?" One of the drunk men near the entrance called over his shoulder. "What does a corpse need food for?" His companions joined in his laughter.

"Shut it, Yostap!" Evpat slammed a mug he was cleaning on the countertop. "At least he pays. If only the living were so generous… You still owe me two kops for last night!"

Yostap shrugged, waved the comment away. "Yeah, yeah." He took a pull from his mug and turned back to his table. "You'll get it." Chairs screeched as hushed conversations resumed.

Leaning back, the mercenary lifted his head and sighed. *The usual.* Izrak's dead gaze drifted towards the ceiling as his thumb ran over the rough, woven pouch at his hip. *Maybe I have lingered here for too long….*

Floorboards whined under the approach of soft footfalls. Izrak looked down. A delicate figure, hooded and cloaked in black, stood at the other side of the table. A pair of ivory hands emerged from beneath the cloak and, as spirits dancing in mist, she signed: *May I sit?*

"You do not have to ask, Olesia." She nodded beneath the hood and sat. Izrak looked upon her for a moment. "They still have not restored your voice, even after all this time?"

They do not forgive. You know their punishments are severe. A century is nothing to them. Though it is rather fitting, is it not? A puppet… without a voice of her own.

Izrak's fingers bit into the sodden wood of the table—fangs sinking into flesh. "I will find a way to restore your voice. I owe you that much."

Yemor deserved to die. I regret nothing. You do not owe me a thing, Ferryman.

The mercenary released his grip. "What tidings then, does an Omen bring?"

Olesia lowered her hood. The Omen's feathered waves of raven hair shimmered in the torchlight, bound at the crown with a silver circlet, a rich amethyst at its center glittering upon her porcelain brow. Her ashen eyes were storms, roiling clouds streaked with flecks of violet lightning. The corners of her mauve lips curled upward as she drew a single bronze coin from the folds of her sleeve. The coin's face bore a gaunt visage, gazing upwards in agony, with gnarled fingers clawing at the cheeks as its tongue hung limp over a pointed chin.

The Omen set the coin in front of him. *Death.*

A Coin of Akheron only meant one thing to the undead slaves of The Call. A rogue warrior, a damned soul whose passage over the River had been purchased with their disobedience and treachery. Izrak took the coin. "Who?"

The Black Bear.

"Zheso Strakh… I suppose it was always a matter of time." Izrak placed the coin in the hidden pocket of his satchel, its soft clink a death knell as it joined the other four. "So be it." The mercenary stood, clasped his sword to his belt.

Olesia rose from her seat. *He was last sighted leaving Ryaz, not two days past, heading south into the Shuvo. Perhaps you may pick up his trail in the forest.*

With a parting smile, Olesia lifted her hood, her spectral face shrouded in shadow once more. She rose, and darkness seethed around her as the torchlight flickered, then dimmed, covering the tavern like a pall. All sound faded to a distant whisper. Then, the creeping shadows collapsed back into the center, and the Omen was gone. The patrons of the Soul's Lament peered about, eyes narrowed, scratching their heads, as though waking from sleep.

The mercenary looked at the old barkeeper as he was heading into the kitchen. "Never mind the food, Evpat." Izrak left three kops on the table and moved towards the entrance.

Evpat spun about. "But Avdoya just finished cutting the pork. What shall I do with it?"

A flash of lightning silhouetted Izrak as he opened the door. Heedless of the rain pouring in through the portal, he glanced back over his shoulder at the vagrants. "Feed it to the dogs. For they will not have my bones to gnaw upon." Prowling winds howled, and the mercenary stepped out into the storm.

I

A PATH FORSAKEN

A crimson dawn bled into the pale blue of a waking sky. Terrible in its majesty, the endless expanse of the heavens was clothed in royal raiment of topaz, ruby, and sapphire, adorned with a rubrous crown of burnished gold. In the valley below, stirred by the gentle caress of night's final breath, the emerald shrouds of ancient pine, oak, aspen, and birch huddled close together, whispering amongst each other of eldritch secrets not meant for the ears of mortal men. And so it was, as Izrak Laav passed among their creaking boles, that he listened and drifted quietly through the arcane realm of Shuvo.

* * *

As the sun reached its zenith, the mercenary came to the crossroads of the merchant road, its broad lane furrowed with deep ruts and littered with the detritus of

Enostran's ever-transient purveyors. Izrak
peered at the twisted signpost stooping over the
junction. Less than a league to the southeast
lay the forest city of Novogor, and to the west,
the Old City, whose name had long faded from
memory.

The main road continued south to the
port city of Sevast. Built from the ruins of
an ancient sea fort, Sevast's high walls and
crenellated battlements, as well as the restricted
access provided by towering cliffs on either side
of the harbor, offered protection to the exiles
and corsairs who sought refuge there. Control
of Sevast was ephemeral, the city wild and
violent, knowing no true master. *Just like him.*

Izrak adjusted his cap, slipped on thick
black-leather gloves, and pulled the hood of his
cloak overhead. He continued south along the
main road.

The mercenary had walked about a mile
when a phantom memory flitted by on the
periphery of his vision. He stopped, turned to
face it, his hand moving for his sword. But his
hand fell away when he saw the girl. No more
than thirteen, her flaxen tresses were tangled,
her hazel eyes wide with terror. *I know you…
I have seen your face.* Beads of crimson trickled
from scratches marring her ruddy cheeks.
Billowing in the breeze, the girl's soiled white

shift was in tatters, her feet caked in mud.
Why is she here? Izrak stepped forward. The girl
staggered back, then turned and ran. *Why does
she flee?*

"Wait—" Just as the mercenary called out,
a gale tore through the trees, lifting dead leaves
and sprigs from the ground in a whirlwind
around him, obscuring his sight. He tried
to break away from the verdant barrier but
was held fast. Looking down, Izrak saw roots
churning the dirt at his feet, wrapping around
his boots. *What devilry is this?* And just as
quickly, the gale dissipated as the leaves drifted
to the loam, and the roots crept back into the
earth. The girl was gone.

The baying of hounds resounded in the
woods behind him, followed soon by the
shouts of several men as they approached. A
pair of black hounds broke through the line
of pines hedging the road. Izrak stood still,
hand resting on his sword. Baying turned to
low growls as the hounds stalked closer, then
whined as they realized what he was, suddenly
backing away.

A middle-aged man, with grizzled hair
in a rough-spun tunic beneath a leather vest,
stepped onto the road. He was quickly joined
by two young men in similar garb, one blonde,
the other red of hair; their eyes glinted with

malice, and cruel smiles split their ruddy faces. All were armed with short swords. The hounds circled behind them and stood with hunched bodies trembling.

The older man glanced at the blonde. "What's with the dogs?" The blonde shrugged his shoulders. Grunting, the older man looked back at Izrak. "Listen, friend. Did you see a girl pass you by on the road? Or in the trees?" His voice was strained, tinged with fear. His eyes narrowed; beads of sweat rolled over his creased brow. "Well?"

Izrak said nothing.

"Are you touched? Matvan asked you a question." The red head sauntered forward, poised to draw his sword. "Did you see a girl?"

"Maybe he didn't, Vasi," the blonde said as he stepped around to the middle of the road, cutting the mercenary off.

Vasi chuckled. "Sure, Resh. Or maybe the fool's hiding her." He pulled his blade. "We'll make him talk. One way or another."

Leather whined as Izrak's grip tightened around his own sword. Vasi lunged. The mercenary's blade flashed from its scabbard, and Izrak stepped to the side, parrying. Vasi stumbled past him. The same instant, Resh charged, sword raised. He thrust. Izrak shifted, avoiding the strike, sending his fist crashing into the man's face at the same moment. Resh went sprawling at Matvan's feet. Vasi recovered and rushed Izrak from behind. The mercenary took a step to the left, evading his overhead blow. The mercenary hooked the man's arms and threw him over his shoulder. Vasi crashed face up into the dirt. Before he could move, Izrak pressed the point of his blade to Vasi's chest, just above the heart.

Resh climbed to his feet, blood oozing from his split lips, and inched forward. Izrak lowered his hood. Resh faltered as the color drained from his face.

Matvan seized him by the shoulder. "Enough! Both of you!" He pulled Resh behind him, turned back to the mercenary. "Forgive my foolish sons. Please, let him go."

Izrak lifted his sword, and Vasi scrambled over to his father. "They would do well to refrain from assaulting strangers on the road." He sheathed his sword. "What is this all about?"

Matvan furrowed his brow, glared at the two men huddled by the hounds. He looked at the mercenary and pointed a shivering thumb over his shoulder. "We're from Novogor. My… daughter, Elishei, ran away just before dawn.

We've been searching for her all morning. She has long blonde hair, hazel eyes. Dressed in white. Tell me you've seen her?"

"With these hounds and those swords, one would think you were hunting the girl."

"There are many dangers in the forest. Wolves. Bears. And darker things…" Matvan cleared his throat. "They're only meant for our protection."

"I see." Izrak's hollow gaze lingered on the men for a moment. He closed his fingers around the pouch on his belt. "Yes, I saw her. Just before you came upon me. Fleeing west."

Baring his teeth, Vasi growled. "Damned corpse! Why didn't you just say so?"

Matvan cuffed him, grabbed him by the collar, his face going red as he spoke in his ear. He turned back to the mercenary. "Perhaps you might join us. We could use another man. There will be payment, of course."

"No."

"What? Why not?" Resh said through the bloody cloth he pressed to his lips.

"I am engaged in another task." Izrak turned away. "I cannot waste any more time here." He glanced over his shoulder. "Have you seen another of my kind pass through Novogor?"

Resh spat blood at the mercenary's feet.

Izrak moved on along the road. "May you find favor in your search."

The mercenary had not gone far before a swift gale rushed out of the east, heading in the direction of Matvan's small band. Izrak halted, listened. He heard the ferocious baying of the hounds, the shouts of the men, both consumed by a ravenous, preternatural howl.

Stay out of it. Their fate was not his concern. Every second he delayed, Zheso moved further beyond the mercenary's reach. Should he fail in his hunt for the rogue warrior... *There are punishments even the dead may fear.* The hounds had gone silent. Izrak kept moving, the shouts of the men growing desperate. *What difference does it make?* Suddenly, the image of Elishei's terrified face flashed through his mind, and a tremor wracked his desolate soul. *Cila...*

Drawing his sword, Izrak grunted. "Curse it all." He dashed from the road, a phantom passing through the trees. Only the terrified cries of the men remained to guide Izrak's pursuit as he followed them into a glade.

Mangled and torn, the bodies of the hounds lay nearby. Matvan and his sons were huddled together, backs pressed against a large stone outcropping at the far edge of the glade. Vasi held his shoulder, blood streaming down his wounded arm. Resh clutched at gashes on his broad chest. But it was a gray wolf the size of a draft horse that gave even the dead mercenary pause. Slaver seeped from between the wolf's fangs as it stalked closer, the air quavering with its menacing snarls.

With inhuman speed, Izrak charged across the glade, unhindered and silent even in his armor. Lifting his sword, he roared. The wolf snapped massive jaws at him, its yellow eyes blazing with amber fire. Izrak thrust his blade; the wolf ducked its head at the last moment, the strike catching its brow. Izrak's blade clipped the wolf's ear as the savage beast leapt away from him. Lips peeled back in a vicious snarl over fangs long as fingers, hackles bristling as the wolf crouched—a hissing dragon coiling before the attack.

Blade gleaming in the sunlight, the mercenary kept his sword trained on the beast. "Leave. Now. I will find the girl," Izrak said without shifting his gaze.

Resh leaned in towards Matvan. "We can't trust him. When Orved hears of this—"

"Shut your mouth." Matvan's face was scarlet, veins bulging in his neck. He looked at Izrak. "We can help you."

"Your sons are wounded. They will need your help to get back. Unless you want to die like your hounds, run." Smoldering embers flared in the pits of Izrak's eyes. "Go!"

Breaking away from the rock, the men ran towards the nearby trees. The monstrous wolf lunged as they fled, but the mercenary stepped in, flashing out his sword and slicing into its muzzle. Shaking its head, the beast growled, then lunged again, snapping its maw shut where Izrak had just been standing. Stepping to the side, the mercenary thrust, plunging his blade through the beast's hide, between its ribs. He struggled to pull it free. *What is this?* Heaving on the sword, it came away coated in a viscous, amber fluid.

With a whine, the wolf staggered back. Then, the hairs of its fur receded, and flesh roiled as howling winds coursed through the glade. The wolf shrank and stood upright upon its hind legs, paws turning to gnarled hands and feet. A man's form took shape. Shrouded in robes of moss and lichen, the figure stood at over seven feet; his skin was bark, dusk-brown, furrowed and thick, with a beard of vines and branches. The eyes were the hollows of an ancient bole, deep and shadowed, set above a broad nose of knotted wood. A wreath of leaves and thorns adorned his crown.

Izrak wiped his blade on his cloak. "Who are you? Why did you attack those men?"

"You intervene in affairs you do not understand. No, this does not concern the dead." The spirit's voice was the rush of wind through autumn boughs.

"Where is Elishei?"

"You cannot save her. Leave this place, or you will never leave it again." The spirit dispersed into a whirlwind of leaves, flowing westward, then vanished among the trees.

Following its course, Izrak chased after the winds. Deep in the forest, trees rustled while branches snapped and groaned; the forest seemed to close in around him. A dense mist rose from the ground, curling around the thick trunks of massive oaks. Vaporous fingers tugged on the mercenary's cloak, grasped at his limbs. His movement became sluggish, strained. Golden sunlight turned to gray haze. He lost all sense of time and direction was lost. An old sensation crept into the mercenary's petrified heart, one primal, that even the dead cannot escape.

Fingers clutching the woven pouch on his belt, Izrak stopped and uttered a prayer his mother had taught him as a child. *She said this prayer would always protect me. Four centuries have failed to prove her false.* Izrak turned around, continued his path.

And the mercenary suddenly found himself back on the merchant road, the afternoon sun shining through the verdant canopy as he stood once more before the signpost at the crossroads. The mist had cleared away, seeping back into the earth. Izrak looked towards a stand of birch just beyond the road, watching the shadows of the trees creep over the loam. *Her path through the woods is lost to me. I will not find her that way.* Shifting his gaze, he looked at the signpost. *The Old City.* One lost could hope to find shelter in those ruins. *Haunted as they may be....*

Cloak billowing on a fell wind, the mercenary set off west along the forsaken path.

II

ONLY ONCE

Faith is patience. Resilient in its timeless endurance, faith remains a steadfast sanctuary for lost and weary wanderers of epochs burdened with strife and discontent. Yet faith is not without tribulation. All must pass through the valley of shadow, where hope is naught but a dim light, a distant memory of halcyon days, long since forgotten. And as the afternoon sun drifted towards uncertain horizons, golden light fading behind a veil of grief-laden clouds, Izrak Laav came upon a church in the outskirts of the Old City.

It was a stout building, despite its age. The log walls yet stood, supporting a terraced roof and large turrets capped with onion-shaped domes. They had been painted with enchanting shades of blue, green, and yellow, but the paint had long since chipped and faded. An eight-pointed cross still gleamed atop the central dome.

The Icon of the Redeemer. The symbol of a foreign religion. *My father's faith.*

Carried on the edge of a sword, the Redeemer's Word had swept through Enostran along with the invading army. The old rulers, and the old gods, fell swiftly. Izrak's father never told him of where he had come from, of his homeland; he claimed that Enostran was his only home. Izrak's mother converted when his parents married and did not speak of his father's past.

Boards whined and creaked as the mercenary ascended the stairs of the church. Sigils of swords, set in relief upon the face of the great iron doors, burned with rust gathered along their edges. He hesitated at the entrance.

Izrak had not set foot inside a church of the Redeemer since he was a young man. *This had been a beautiful place once.* Yet even then, the faith had begun to fail, and the people fell back into the old ways. He pushed against the doors. They opened with ease, and the dead man stepped inside.

Light entered through small cracks in the roof, falling in golden, glimmering shafts across the haze of dust hanging in the air. Warped boards groaned underfoot as Izrak moved into the nave. A soft click sounded from the right. Looking over, the mercenary saw a small door, crooked in its battered frame. Walking over, he took hold of the pitted iron handle. Izrak faltered. *What should I say to her … after all this time?* His grip loosened on the handle. *How can I make her trust me? Again….*

Shaking his head, the mercenary opened the door.

Squealing on its hinges, the door opened into what was once a small office. A bookshelf was set against the left wall, rotten books scattered over broken, dust-coated shelves. A moldering rug, worn and frayed, lay upon the floor. At the far end, windows of stained glass, miraculously preserved, overlooked a writing desk, overturned, lying upon its side. A tarnished candelabrum lay bent and twisted beside it.

Slowly, Izrak approached the desk. He heard it now, just as before: the muffled staccato of strained breaths, the shifting of threadbare cloth over wood, the shuffle of feet pressing a trembling body against the fragile desk that could offer neither shelter nor protection. *Just like that night.*

An umbral mélange fell over the mercenary's mind. Witch-fire smoldered in the pits of his eyes as his jaw quivered. Hand closing around the pouch, Izrak stood petrified. Tremors racked his body as phantom claws tore at his consciousness. *Torn asunder… Torn in two. Torn to pieces. Tearing. Ripping. Feeding….*

Hollow voices called out to him from the periphery of his fading sight; for joy and for pain, out of love and out of hate, they cried out to the dead man. They bled into one voice, faint, terrified, and alone, yet slipped through the woeful chorus—a cold blade into a cold heart. She cried out for help. *She needs you. Go to her. Protect her. Save her!*

Vision suddenly cleared, Izrak took hold of the desk and shoved it aside. And wide, hazel eyes met his shadowed gaze. Flaxen tresses hung in matted strands over cheeks crusted with dried blood. Mud-covered feet thrashed as she tried to back away, but her fear-stricken body refused to respond. Izrak reached out for the girl. Driven beyond desperation, the girl's hand flashed out, seized the candelabrum, then hurled it at him.

Centuries of battle experience had somehow failed the mercenary against such a simple, childish trick. In a parody of self-preservation, he lifted his arm to guard against the projectile. Childish. Simple. But it was enough. The girl was already rushing past him towards the door when the mercenary lowered his arm. Izrak whirled about as she nearly ripped the door out of its frame. "Elishei! Stop!"

At the sound of her name, the girl froze in the doorway, her chest heaving, one hand clutching the handle.

"Please…." Izrak held out his hands, inching closer. "I will not harm you." Another step.

Elishei's eyes flicked to the sword on his belt. A board popped, breaking under his dead weight. She fled; the door slamming shut behind her.

"Elishei!" Izrak charged the door, tearing it from its hinges, flinging it aside as he rushed into the nave. Only the dust remained to receive him. The girl had vanished.

The doors of the narthex remained shut. Izrak was certain he would have seen her leave that way. Assuming Elishei was still within the church, the mercenary entered the nave, his footsteps echoing with haunting resonance throughout the silent chamber as he passed rows of crumbling pews.

A large altar stood before him at the end of the chamber. Providing shelter, a stone ciborium, supported by four pillars, nearly reached the ceiling. The altar's base of carved stone displayed the symbol of the church. Somehow, spots of vibrant color remained, but most of it was now covered in grime or

weathered away. Izrak's fingers played over the
rough fibers of the pouch at his hip as he gazed
upon the altar. *The last time I was here....*

Rusted hinges moaned as the main doors
opened. Izrak's hand moved to his sword as the
rush of soft fabric coursed over the decrepit
planks as a gentle brook. He turned. A skeleton
dressed in white shambled down the aisle.

As it approached, muscles and sinew spread
over the macabre frame from some unseen
center. Long, chocolate locks flowed from the
crown of its skull, weaving into a thick braid
as alabaster flesh materialized over the exposed
tissue. Izrak stood paralyzed as the specter
mounted the altar, taking her place before him.

She looked at him, and her lids closed over
the hollow pits. Opening them once more,
her eyes were honey, warm and sweet. *Lebi. It
cannot be...* Some force pulsed within Izrak's
chest. Only once. And never again.

Lebi smiled, her cheeks flushed—the
bloom of a winter rose.

"Do you remember," her voice a discordant
melody, "the last words you spoke to me?" She
reached out with ghostly fingers, caressing the
sharp bone of Izrak's cheeks. All faded into
darkness.

III

SOMEONE ELSE

Lebi stood in front of the door, her trembling hand hovering over the knob. Nerves fraying at the edges, all she wanted was sleep; yet she feared entering her own bedroom. Lebi's eyes watered as the fetid odor seeping from under the door harried her nose. He was in there. And his rising anger seemed to choke the life out of any space he occupied.

Am I being unfair? After all, he had only been back a few weeks. The ghosts of his years of battle still haunted his mind, broken by his return from death. Lebi sent her husband to war. Someone else came back.

Breathing deep, she opened the door and passed into the room. A pair of candles flickered upon a side table. Beside them rested a woven pouch.

Lebi's languid gaze lingered on its rough-spun, soiled fabric as gooseflesh crawled over her arms and back. She never told him of her nightmare, the one still tormenting her, about the night he returned home: Lebi moved to the front door, drawn by a faint scratching upon its wooden planks; she opened the door, and a being raised from the pits of Hell stumbled over the threshold, the pouch clutched in pallid hands. He uttered a single word, a name…

Starlight spilled in through the window at the end of the room, washing her husband's writing desk in silver hues. And there Izrak sat, clothed in simple garb, thin strands of blonde hair hanging limp from sunken temples. The room was quiet except for the scratching of quill on parchment, and the rattle of breath, bereft of life.

At the sound of the door closing, the scratching ceased for a moment, then continued.

"Cila is in bed. She could not stop talking about her morning with you." Her smile shriveled into a frown. "Ryol still has not come home. I am worried about him. Will you not go look for your son?"

Izrak set down his quill and faced her. "Worry not. Ryol is hardly without protection?"

His hollow gaze chilled her blood. Lebi held herself, rubbing her shoulders. "All he wants is for you to teach him. To be like you."

"Like me…" The dead man turned away. "He should pray such a curse never befalls him. No. My son will never be a soldier."

"That is not for you to decide! Why can you not just—"

Quill and parchment jumped as Izrak's fist slammed against the desk. Lebi started, her heart hammering in her chest. She calmed herself, then moved closer, her hand reaching for Izrak's shoulder. She pulled away.

"Bogda found another of his pigs mutilated this morning. What was left of it, anyway."

Izrak lowered his head in his hands. "Forgive me, Lebi. My hunger grows. Nothing I do seems to sate it." The dead man continued his writing. "And *she* will not tell me what to do. I call out to *her* day after day. Still … *she* refuses to heed me."

Tears welled in her eyes, but Lebi wiped them away.

"I am glad to see you writing again." Peering over his shoulder, she looked to see what he had written. *That name.* Countless times, filling page after page. Lebi sighed, then moved to the table, her gaze fixed upon the pouch. *What does he keep in here?*

"Izrak," she said, reaching for the pouch, "who is Kalis?"

The chair crashed against the wall as Izrak shot to his feet. "Do not touch her!" he roared. His body quivered with unrestrained rage as he approached her.

Lebi blanched, stumbled back onto the bed as the candles flickered out, plunging the room into darkness. She screamed.

The dead man, wreathed in shadow, drew near with hitched steps. His eyes flared orange, pits set with burning coals....

IV

Vision returned to Izrak as he stood upon the altar. Lebi was gone, taking with her whatever warmth had remained to a day growing cold under the weary eye of the late afternoon sun. The dead man fell to his knees. Trembling fingers raked over the stone where she had stood mere moments before—and yet so long ago. His roar reverberated through the chamber, his eyes flaring with hellfire. Stone fractured under the force of his fists crashing against the floor.

Then silence, and Izrak shrank into himself.

Light spilled into the narthex as the iron doors opened once more. Izrak looked over, saw the forest spirit standing just beyond the threshold, before he turned and stepped away from the church. The mercenary climbed to his feet and followed.

Outside, he found the spirit standing beneath a dead willow, its barren branches swaying in the breeze. Hand on the grip of his sword, Izrak approached.

"My realm is no place for the dead. Leave, warrior. Only torment awaits you on this path," the spirit said as he ran his hand over the desiccated bole of the willow.

"Enough games, Old One." Izrak drew his sword, the blade's edges singing with fury. "Where is Elishei?"

"Safe…." the spirit whispered—the susurration of a somber brook. He faced the mercenary. "Would you protect her? And with what? Your sword knows but one song." He looked towards the darkness gathering in the west. "How could you protect anyone… with so much hate?"

Izrak lowered his blade, looked upon edges nicked and worn by countless battles. *It never ends. And for what?* The mercenary shifted his dead gaze to the willow, watching as its long arms raked over withered grass and parched soil. *It all ends the same way….*

"Your emptiness knows only hunger. Your hate only consumes." Dissipating into a whirlwind, the spirit coursed through the air, racing westward. His last words were a murmur on the wind. "You cannot save her."

Izrak slammed his sword back into its scabbard.

Damn it all! He grasped at the woven pouch. *Why did you do this to me? Why will you not let me rest?* "Answer me!"

Only the echoes of his wrath offered reply.

This is my punishment. The mercenary peered back at the church. *There is no forgiveness.* Izrak returned to the path, continuing his tired trudge to the Old City. *For what I did to you....*

* * *

Night unfurled over the valley upon sable dragon wings. Serpent shadows coiled beneath the sanguine veil of the sun's dying light. Jagged pines rose along undulating hills like spines over the infernal line of the horizon, and the lofty boughs of birch flared upon the pyre of day's passing. Dusk's tenebrous fingers crept from the pines shouldering the root-choked path, reaching in blind, ravenous desire to ensnare the wretched and forlorn. Driven by despair, he passed into a chthonic realm lost beneath the depths of eons unfathomable, where death was not an end, but another state of being. And thus, as the moon rose from the ashes of a dead sun, did Izrak Laav find himself at the Stygian shores of the Old City.

And the mercenary trembled at the sight. Spread over the valley floor as an infection through a wound, the Old City was a black abomination. Obsidian obelisks towered hundreds of feet over the city, their jewel-encrusted tips glimmering in provocation to the stars above. Cyclopean spires rose in magnificent decadence among domed monoliths of alien dimensions. At the nexus of the blasphemous city lay a coliseum seated upon a terraced pyramid, a great stair cutting a swath up to the threshold of the dread arena. The Algov flowed down from the eastern mountains, through the city, where it fed a somnolent lake gleaming beneath the moonlight—a portal to an argent plane of dreams eternal.

Whatever sort of madness could drive the girl to this place was almost incomprehensible to the mercenary. *Yet, this is where the path has led me…* Izrak's gaze was drawn once more to the terrible coliseum. *I must see it through… For her.*

Releasing the pouch at his hip, the mercenary began his descent into the city.

* * *

A gibbous moon approached its zenith as Izrak climbed the final step and emerged onto a vast courtyard before the gates of the coliseum. Like a still lake, its mirrored surface glowed faintly under the ghost-light of the stars. Hundreds of black sculptures, as though scorched, melted, knelt throughout the court with arms outstretched. Their carven faces, contorted with misery and pain, were lifted in blind supplication to a monstrous statue of a three-headed dragon, an image of a dark god of the old world. *Garyn'zmei.*

Izrak recognized the great serpent from the legends his mother had told him on brumal nights, seated before the warm light of a blazing hearth.

Born from the primordial reaches of the Vnesh'tot, the Outer Void, at the dawn of creation, Garyn'zmei was not simply evil; the serpent was chaos incarnate. Evil paid tribute to him. Tales of the horrid dragon never failed to frighten the young Izrak, and even now, his image gave the mercenary pause. The implications of the idol's presence in the city were more than he dared to dwell upon.

After a moment, the mercenary moved on to the gates of the coliseum.

Sand crunched under his boots as Izrak stepped into the arena. In the shape of a hexagon, its vacant galleries climbed to a domed roof that was open at the apex. The silver eye of the moon peered through, a cosmic spectator plagued by boredom, and unscrupulous in the application of its remedy. Umbral pillars of liquid shadow flanked the perimeter of the battleground, heaved upon the backs of skeletal men, faces twisted in agony under the crushing weight of their perdurable burdens. Scaled serpents coiled over the pillars, their heads slithering over the tops to gaze upon the abhorrent spectacles that were once on display.

"Elishei!" Izrak called out as he moved to the center. *Please*. "Elishei!"

"She's not here." The mocking voice, smooth, cruel, seethed from the shadows behind.

The mercenary spun about, his blade an argent gleam as Izrak drew it. A man, a warrior, leaned against the base of an adjacent pillar, his head resting upon the shoulder of the forsaken soul.

He wore a cuirass of black scales over a shirt of mail, vambraces and greaves of burnished steel, and dark pauldrons in the shape of dragon's heads. Crowned with a silver circlet adorned with a dragon head, its wings wrapped around his temples, the warrior was the image of the great serpent made man.

Stepping away, he moved to join Izrak at the center. "It's just you," he said, lifting his longsword, holding the point level with the mercenary, "and me."

Standing a head taller than Izrak, his hair was dusk-brown, eyes the color of aged amber. *Just like his mother…* Cheeks sloped down at hard angles to deep lines around the mouth. A full beard and furrowed brow aged him ten summers, but there was no mistaking the man's identity.

"Ryol…."

Ryol sneered. "Father."

Izrak stepped towards his son. "How is this possible?"

"Does it matter? Four hundred years I've waited to put you in the ground. You had your chance to talk." Ryol shifted stance. "Now, you're going to listen."

Before Izrak had processed the words, a heavy boot slammed into his chest, sending the mercenary reeling. Instinct took over, and he recovered as Ryol closed the distance, narrowly avoiding the dark warrior's cross slash.

Ryol thrust, driving his blade at the mercenary's skull. Izrak parried the strike, countered with an overhead blow. Catching the slash with ease, Ryol shifted his blade, pulling Izrak's sword down with his crossguard. Thrown off balance, the mercenary lurched forward just as the pommel of Ryol's sword crashed into his face. Izrak went sprawling.

The dark warrior charged in with an overhead stroke that sank into the sand, just missing Izrak as he rolled away. Jumping to his feet, the mercenary thrust his blade at Ryol's throat. Ryol parried, then drove Izrak back under a flurry of titanic blows that strained the limits of the mercenary's preternatural strength.

Ryol swatted his father's sword aside, grabbed him by the throat, and lifted him bodily from the ground. "Is this what I looked up to!" he roared through bared teeth. The warrior hurled Izrak several feet into the sand, a child discarding an unwanted toy.

The mercenary rolled to a crouch, but Ryol was already upon him before he could stand, the dark warrior's blade falling in a shimmering arc. Izrak lifted his sword overhead in desperate defense. Ryol's cleaved through Izrak's battered weapon, the shards of the blade showering the mercenary as he tumbled back onto his knees.

Izrak looked at the hilt of his shattered sword. *Is that what I have become?* It fell from his hand as he gazed at his son.

"All I ever wanted was to be you," Ryol said, his back turned to the mercenary. "All I wanted was for you to teach me to fight. To be strong!" He faced him, eyes dark with contempt. "As you were. Once."

Izrak's head sank to his chest. "I wanted a different life for you. A life of peace."

"Look at me, father." Izrak lifted his head. Ryol held his blade before him. "Do you remember this sword?"

My old sword… given to me by my father. Izrak looked away.

"You should've taught me to use it," Ryol said, lifting his weapon overhead. "I could have saved her then. Saved her from you."

Izrak looked up once more, watched as the blade fell towards him. Each second was a lifetime in passing. *How it should have ended…* His vision flashed silver under the gleam of the blade. All faded into darkness.

V

ALL THAT WAS GOOD AND RIGHT

Ryol retreated into the shade of the main room, the cut on his cheek still burning.

Slicing potatoes for the evening stew, his mother stood before a steaming pot; the hearty aroma never failed to bring a hungry growl to the boy's stomach. *Cila must be playing outside.* Seated at the table in the center of the room, his father ran a cloth, damp with oil, over his sword.

Ryol's eyes lingered on the blade, peering at the arcane sigils engraved along the length of the fuller. The boy had often asked what those sigils meant. A sacred oath? An ancient spell? His father never told him. It was a secret. Just like everything else about Izrak Laav.

Placing a small crate of writing materials— fresh quills and parchment—near the door, Ryol moved to the table as Izrak poured more oil onto the cloth, and without looking up, resumed his work.

"I'm back, father." Ryol grimaced as he ran a finger over his cut.

Izrak handled the longsword with ease, as though it were another quill in his pallid hands. "Was Pisat able to supply what I requested?"

"Yes, father. He even discounted the price." Ryol held out a pair of kops. "Here." His father placed the cloth on the table and looked at him. Those hollow eyes… As gazing into a starless sky in the dead of night, Ryol's head swam in the abyss of that desolate stare.

Izrak examined the coins for a moment, then stood. "They are yours. You have earned them." He turned and stepped over to the unlit hearth. On hooks mounted above the fireplace, the dead man hung his father's sword.

"Thank you, father." The boy returned the coins to his jacket pocket.

Izrak moved to stand before him. Ryol lowered his head, nose wrinkled, lips pinched, resisting the urge to back away. *It's not his fault.* Even now, he loved his father—*what's left of him*—but the smell; it was getting worse. Composing his face, he looked up. The dead man traced a cold thumb over the cut. Ryol's gut roiled.

"What happened?"

Ryol glanced at his mother. Knuckles pressed to her lips, Lebi's eyes darted to Izrak, then back to Ryol. He looked back at his father.

"I passed some of the other boys from the village on my way home. They were practicing with their training swords near the river. Father, I didn't mean to, but Andri, Bogda's son, insulted you. And the things he said about mother... I told him to take back his words. Said he would if I could beat him in a duel."

"Did you defeat him?"

A tear rolled over Ryol's cheek just before he wiped it away. His head fell.

"You have nearly sixteen summers to your name, yet you deign to squabble with the others as a child." Izrak pushed past the boy to the entryway.

Face flushed, Ryol spun about. "If you would've taught me how to fight, I could've won! I could've defended my mother's honor. And yours!"

"And do their words cut so deep," the dead man lifted the crate near the door, "that you would place yourself in danger to avenge them?"

"What do you know about it?" Ryol's face twisted, his eyes blazing with fury.

His mother blanched. "Ryol! Do not—"

Izrak lifted a hand. "Let the boy speak, Lebi."

"You never leave the house. You don't hear what they say about us. About you! They tease Cila at the market with mother. Everyone mocks me behind my back. I can't take it anymore!" Ryol's chest heaved as a turgid silence settled over the room.

Izrak stared at the boy for a moment.

"And if I teach you the arts of the sword, then what? You will slay every man, woman, and child who bears an ill word upon their tongue?"

"No, father. I just…" Ryol looked at the sword on the wall, "I want to feel like I can do something. I'm scared. You don't hear what they say…."

"I hear enough." Izrak moved beside him, gazing at his father's sword. "War has plagued our family for generations, a disease passed on from father to son." He looked at Ryol and placed a hand upon his shoulder. "Though your grandfather taught me the ways of war, I vowed I would never become a soldier. I failed to keep that vow. Yet you have a chance for something more. Something good." The dead man sighed. "Come with me. I will share the skills I learned from my mother, to make ink and illuminate texts."

Ryol shrugged off his father's hand. "I don't want to be a scribe! I want to protect my family. Defend my home." The boy rushed over to the fireplace. "If you won't teach me how, I'll teach myself." Lifting the sword from the wall, Ryol faced his father. "If you won't protect our family," he said, charging out the door, "I will!"

* * *

Awash in the starlight, the grove glowed silver and pulsed with the ferocity of his nocturnal assault. The chill night air did little to cool Ryol's blazing passions. The would-be warrior attacked mercilessly, imitating the forms he had spent hours watching the other boys practicing, and hacked at the besieged branches of a defenseless willow.

Heavy in his sweat-slicked hand, the weight of the sword felt good. It was power; power that he could wield, that he could control. How could his father not understand? Ryol knew, felt in his soul, that this was what he was meant to be, a hero, in helm and armor with sword in hand, a protector of all that was good and right.

Ryol switched stance, stepped in for another strike when a scream pierced the veil of night's charnel shroud. The boy froze mid-swing, whirled about. *Was that...* Another scream tore through the air. A tremor jolted through Ryol, his spine going rigid. *Mother!*

Crashing through the thin boles of aged aspen, Ryol raced towards the source of the chilling scream, towards his home. Charging into the dooryard, he saw the house had fallen into darkness, a dread silence hanging over the home—the silence just before a sentence is passed.

A battering ram at the gates, Ryol's heart hammered against his chest as he stepped inside, caution hindering his advance like volleys of arrows from the ramparts. Inside, the air was ice, his breath a mist as he moved through the main room. Shadows seemed to writhe in the corners and under the low spaces, crawling out, heedless of the moon's futile attempts to drive them back. *What is this cold? This dark... Not natural.* The boy crept into a narrow hall.

"Mother? Father?" Ryol whispered, holding the sword in front of him as he neared the bedrooms.

A scuffing sound, wood against wood, sounded from the room to his left. *Cila!* He burst into his sister's room. Her bed lay empty, the fur covers splayed over the floor. *No. Where is she?* Something shifted under the bed. "Cila!" Just then, a squelching sound— fingers churning raw meat—seethed from their parents' room. Despair seized his throat, dragged him to their door. It stood slightly ajar. Ryol peered inside.

Illuminated by the frail light of a helpless moon, the boy saw a figure crouched over another on the bed. Ryol's eyes widened as he met his mother's listless gaze. Rage overpowered terror as he thrust the door open, leapt inside, sword raised.

"What have you done? Get away from her!"

Izrak ceased his feeding, his body still as death. The dead man's head turned slowly over his shoulder, lipless maw glistening crimson. His eyes flared orange, pits set with burning coals....

VI

IT OPENS FROM WITHIN

Vision returned to Izrak as he knelt before his executioner. A broken blade lay upon the sand. *My son.* The mercenary looked up.

Ryol kneeled before him, leaning on his grandfather's sword, its edges dull and rusted, the sigils along the fuller now faded. No longer the dark warrior, Ryol was once again the image of a boy, no more than sixteen. *As you were… so long ago.* Staring at Izrak, the boy remained silent.

Izrak reached out a trembling hand. Ryol's flesh began to fall away in flakes of ashen decay, his body withering as thew and bone crumbled into dust. The boy slumped forward as his sword disintegrated in a cloud of rust. Still, his gaze was fixed upon the mercenary, honeyed eyes fading to milk-white.

"This is your legacy, Izrak Laav." Ryol's voice was distant, empty. "This is all that you have left behind."

"Ryol!" Izrak lurched forward, grasping for the boy as the last remnants of the revenant collapsed into a ruinous heap. "No!" Leaning over, his fingers sank into the mound. "I am sorry... Please."

Moaning from beyond the shadows, a phantom wind stole through the coliseum. Ash, dust and sand, sifted through the dead man's fingers—a murmur of cold lament—as Ryol's remains rose in a whirlwind, drifted back, then reformed into the shape of a man.

A feral snarl escaped Izrak as the forest spirit materialized before him. Climbing to a bestial crouch, the dead man's eyes were ablaze with hellfire.

"Where is he?" Chainmail rattled as the dead man's body quaked with rage. "Give him back to me!" Izrak's roar thundered through the arena. "Give me my son!"

"Ryol is lost to you, warrior," the spirit said, pointing a gnarled finger at Izrak. "By your own hand, your son is dead, consumed by the very wrath that burns within you, even now." He lowered his hand. "Your son will never return."

Izrak's movement was a blur as he charged the spirit, maw agape with ravenous hunger. The dead man would have answers, even if he had to tear them from the spirit piece by piece.

Just as Izrak reached him, the spirit dissipated into a whirlwind. Grains of sand lashed at leather, mail, and bone as the dead man was lifted from the ground on a furious gale and hurled against a pillar. Stunned by the force of the impact, Izrak slumped to the ground, the unholy fire of his eyes extinguished.

Supporting himself on the pillar, the dead man climbed to his feet. Fierce winds howled as they coursed throughout the arena. One hand holding his head, Izrak clutched at the pouch on his belt. *Why do you do this to me? Why will you not let her go?*

The winds gathered rapidly in the center of the coliseum. "You do this to yourself, Izrak Laav." Roiling columns of air rushed upwards to the starlit oculus, the spirit's voice a faint echo on the rising currents. "Leave, warrior. You cannot save her…."

Then the air was still. And the Old City was shrouded in silence once more.

Izrak gazed at the haunted face of the moon, studying its terrible expanse of ivory

desolation, its umbral seas of ebony despair.
The dead man wanted desperately to crawl
beneath the sands of the arena, to hide in that
blood-soaked darkness until time itself ceased
to pass, and all matter, all thought, dissolved
into the icy embrace of oblivion. *Is this not
where I belong?* A silver glint drew his gaze to
the wind-whipped sands; his broken blade still
lay where it had fallen. *Is this not all that I am?*

Fingers closing on the pouch at his hip,
Izrak faced the gates of the coliseum. *What do
you want me to do? How long must I endure this
suffering?*

After a moment, the mercenary released
the pouch and passed through the gates. *You
cannot save her.* The spirit's words haunted his
mind as Izrak stepped out into the courtyard.
Facing south, he wondered if the Old One
was right. Rescuing Elishei would not make a
difference. *It will not bring her back.* Hunting
Zheso provided a clear purpose, one that the
mercenary understood. *There is no forgiveness.*
Izrak moved towards the pyramid stairs. *Only
vengeance.*

As he reached the stairs, Elishei's face—*her
face*—once again seared his consciousness.

Izrak froze and looked to the east. *Is that
all there is? Only vengeance? Four hundred years
I have followed this path. Four hundred years*

*I have walked through the fire, passed through shadow. I have slain man and monster, noble and peasant. I have travelled the length and breadth of this land in search of its mysteries, that I might attain my final wish. Yet four hundred years of strife have not granted me that which I seek...
Only that which I deserve.*

Hunger... Ceaseless hunger...

A sudden flash of white, like an alabaster flame, flickered in the deserted avenues below. Izrak could make out the image of a young girl, flitting between the shadows of the monstrous edifices flanking the streets, racing towards the western reaches of the city.

Hunger burned within his desiccated guts, lashed at his back with fiery whips. He lurched towards the stairs, and with hitched steps, the dead man began his shambling descent.

* * *

Elishei was lost.

Sweat-slicked fingers tightened on the branch she had scavenged from the forest after fleeing the church. It was a poor weapon, but what more could an orphan expect? Elishei gazed upon the branch, wondering what it might possibly do to stop the demons that hunted her. *Would it even make a difference?*

She peered around the corner of a monstrous black monolith, the dead silence of the city weighing on her like the unthinkable mass of alien stone towering above her. Elishei felt small. *Why me? Why us?* The road ahead looked the same as the last.

Clinging to the mocking shadows, she rounded the corner, sidled along the wall. *Grigor would know how to get out of here.* Elishei missed her brother. She missed *him* too. She just wished Gromm had been able to free them both. *But I'll find help. I'll find a way to get them out. All of them.*

Pain shot through her bleeding feet, and tears welled in her eyes. She needed a place to rest.

A roaring wind tore through the silence of the city. Eyes wide, Elishei saw a whirlwind rising out from that terrible arena in the city's center. The roiling column rose higher, stopped, lingered for a moment as tendrils of air spread out like fingers searching. Then they folded back in, and the whirlwind shot through the sky, heading towards her.

The wind coursed along the avenue, its cool touch soothing her aching body, and pulled at her limbs, urging her forward. A voice came to her, a mountain spring, rising from the depths of her mind.

"Follow me, child. I will show you the way…"

Elishei pressed her back to the wall. *What are you?*

"A friend… Now, quickly. They draw near, and I cannot remain here much longer."

For an instant, she hesitated, then chased after her ethereal guide.

A series of rapid turns carried Elishei through the labyrinthine streets at a breathless pace. Chest heaving, the girl rounded another dusk-haunted corner. Elishei winced at the sharp pain in her feet. The winds whispered to her.

"A little farther, child. We are near the edge of the city. Another right turn, up ahead, will lead you out to the safety of the forest."

Lancing pain seared the soles of her feet, and Elishei sprawled across the ground. The branch tumbled from her hand, rolling a short distance ahead. Panting, she rolled to her back, peered down the street into the moonlit gloom. A low snarling prowled the shadows beyond, crept towards her as three pairs of gleaming yellow orbs appeared.

Elishei sobbed, rolled over, and scrambled for the branch. Seizing it, she leapt to her feet, faced the yellow orbs once more. The snarling grew louder as she backed away. Several long claws emerged from the black. Her breath caught in her throat; she trembled as her skin crawled with spiders of ice. The snarls deepened into growls, then, suddenly, pitched to whines. Elishei started breathing again as the claws retreated, and the yellow orbs blinked out.

What happened? Elishei staggered back a step. *It doesn't matter.* She looked over her shoulder. The next corner was at hand. *I need to go!* The girl spun around, about to run.

And gloved fingers curled around the edge of the structure. Elishei cried out as she slid to a stop. With hitched movements, the dead man rounded the corner, hellfire smoldering in the pits of his eyes. Mouth parting, his lipless grin seemed to grow a little wider.

The dead man staggered forward, reached out for her. Elishei backed away, holding the branch before her like a sword. Halting, his burning eyes dimmed, and the dead man reeled back, clutching his skull.

"No... No! I never meant to..." The dead man growled, pressed his hands to his face. He peered at her through his fingers. "You look like her. As she was... back then." Snarling, he hunched over, still clutching his face.

Elishei took another step back, lifted the branch above her shoulder.

The dead man's gaze snapped to her, eyes blazing. Roaring, he lunged for the girl.

Wood split against his skull as Elishei swung with all the strength she possessed, stunning him for an instant. She ducked under his outstretched arms, slipped past him, and raced along the avenue.

As the dead man turned to face her, Elishei was already clear of the Old City. She risked one look back. He shambled after her, calling out a name. Only the cries of the dead man remained to pursue her as she crashed through the trees, the name an echo in her mind.

And though Elishei dared not stop to ponder, she could not but wonder who she was to him. *Who is Cila?*

* * *

A soul can only withstand so much punishment. Even less the soul that is fractured, weary, corrupted beyond all reconciliation, and the smallest mercy becomes a searing brand. And the brand leaves its mark upon the condemned; kindness turns to insult, love inflicts torture, and forgiveness becomes a prison for the unhallowed dead. Within that prison, the dead man lingers, languishes, and hope bleeds slowly through the black iron bars of a lonesome cell, until at last, despair guides his thoughts towards desperate escape. Yet, escape is but an empty grave. Night after night, he dreams of the grave's dark embrace, of its cold oblivion, all the while failing to discern that the cell door was never locked, and that it opens from within….

And as a damned soul crawling out from the black depths of perdition, the dead man shambled towards the expanding ring of coruscant light piercing the dense line of birch screening the lake. He hesitated. Uncertain of what he may find on the other side of that verdant veil, doubt hunched his back as Izrak stood ensnared, hands held out before his face—the pulsating light was blinding to the dead man's unholy sight—a shameful pariah, clutching the rusted bars of his darkling cell.

Yet, there was nothing left. *She* was without, waiting on the other side.

Grasping the pouch on his hip, the dead man pushed through the boles.

Izrak emerged and stood at the edge of a clearing. *Where are you?* The light had vanished. Blades of soft green grass swayed in rhythmic undulations with the breeze, the leaves of the trees sighing as though in deep slumber. He moved into the clearing.

A large windmill towered overhead to the right, resting upon a square structure of ancient logs. Part of the roof had fallen in. Its broken sails turned slowly on the gathering winds.

Further ahead, a field of white lilies, possessed of an unnatural luminescence, circled the shore of the vast lake. The water was still, the night sky reflected in its surface, spreading beyond the mist-veiled horizon. It was as though the dead man were standing at the edge of the world, gazing out into the brumal expanse of frost-limned eternity….

How often had Izrak found himself here? Back turned towards a world fraught with strife and deceit, standing at the edge of an infinite and unknowable truth. Unknowable, forever at the tips of his fingers, forever out of reach. Yet he wanders, the soles of his boots flayed by his torturous pilgrimage; he peels back the earth's flesh, digging, clawing, cruelly seeking the secrets of creation's eldritch mysteries, only to find that the question is pointless, for the answer is always the same. Always the same.

Where are you?

Sweet laughter… "I'm here, Papa."

A tremor wracked the dead man's desolate frame, shattered the smothering fugue of his suffocating mind.

A young girl of seven summers stood before him at the water's edge, facing away, her pearlescent nightgown billowing over the water like the morning mist. She turned and looked up at him. Her image was dawn in the heart of spring; fair, blonde tresses flowed in resplendent golden rays down her shoulders, around a soft face white as clouds, over eyes like dew-frosted meadows glistening beneath the rising sun. *Cila*....

Izrak staggered, fell to his knees. "Daughter..." The dead man trembled, arms hanging at his sides, fingers digging into the soil, seeking for something real to hold onto, to assuage the anguish of a grieving soul. "Forgive me... Please, do not leave me." He lifted his hollow gaze to her. Black ichor, profane tears, seethed from the purulent pits. "Forgive me."

Cila smiled. "I never left you, Papa." She woke one of the budding lilies from its bed, plucked it, and stepped closer to her father. Tracing the edges of the petals with her finger, she said, "I think forgiveness is like one of these." Taking the dead man's hand, she placed the flower on his soiled palm. "It's a gift." She closed his fingers around the bud. "It's selfish to keep it to yourself." Holding Izrak's hand, she knelt before him. "Can you forgive yourself, Papa?"

The dead man lifted his empty hand towards Cila, brushed her cheek, then pulled back. Izrak looked away. "How could I?"

The girl giggled. "I told you, Papa. Like the flower. It's a gift, but you need to take care of it. Give it warmth and love and room to grow. You decide what to do with it." Cila lifted her father's hand. "Look."

Izrak opened his hand. The lily was in full bloom, diamond petals shimmering with radiant splendor.

"Just like that flower, Papa. It opens from within." Cila reached out, held the dead man's head, and wiped the black tears from her father's eyes. All faded into darkness.

VII

WE WILL GO TOGETHER

Cila stepped out onto the riverbank, a faint song of spring upon her lips.

The skirt of her sarafan danced lightly on the morning breeze. Verdant boughs swayed overhead in rhythm to the azure, crystalline hum of the rolling waters; the descant tones of nightingales warbled harmoniously with the child's sanguine melodies. Vitality surged within the sturdy boles of aspen and birch, and illuminated the petals of plantain, iris, and loosestrife in a tableau of chromatic splendor.

All about her, creation rose in concert, celebrating the birth of a new season, singing praise for new beginnings. And as the girl moved into a neighboring grove, to pick mushrooms for her mother, Cila offered silent prayers for the rebirth of dreams once lost to the dead of winter.

It was not long before Cila's basket was nearly full of brown porcini and golden chanterelles. *Mama's stew will be so tasty*! She grinned as she placed another chanterelle inside, breathing deep its sweet apricot scent. *Maybe Papa will eat with us too…* Yet, Cila's smile shriveled as another scent sought to overpower it, one decadent, foul, and out of place in her floral haven.

The odor grew stronger.

Holding the ends of her shawl to her nose, Cila turned about. The birds had ceased their singing, and the sunlight seemed to retreat from an umbral patch of dense, twisted brush across the grove. Warmth fled from her; the girl's skin crawled as she pressed her back against a tall birch. Underbrush crunched; branches snapped. Cila held the basket to her chest.

A pale hand broke through the dark, twisted mass, then another, and pulled it apart. And Izrak Laav emerged into the grove. Cila stood frozen, watching as her father—*the dead man*—approached, his darkling eyes fixed upon her.

"Cila?" Izrak halted a few paces away. "Did something frighten you, daughter?" Taking another step, he gestured to the basket. "You have gathered so many. Your mother will be pleased. Still, I thought I might join you."

Daughter… Cila remained silent. Even still, she was unaccustomed to her father's presence.

Just an infant when he left, the girl had little sense of who or what he was, only that which her mother and brother had seldom spoken of. *I wish I remembered how you looked… before.* Cila stared at the dead man, scoured the empty eyes, the sad smile, the tiny fissures lining the bones of his face, like wrinkles in the skin he no longer wore, searching for some semblance of the father she never knew.

Cila looked away. "Yes, Papa." Her voice was muffled beneath the shawl. "Let's go back to the river. The air is sweeter there."

"As you wish. And how may I help?"

Giggling, Cila released her shawl and thrust out the fungal hoard. "You get to carry the basket!"

Izrak chuckled, took the basket. "So be it."

The sun climbed towards noon, and with her father's aid, Cila filled the basket to near overflowing. After adding a particularly large bay bolete to the gathering, Izrak moved down the embankment near the water and sat upon the grass. He placed a hand beside him. "Come, Cila. Sit with me."

Joining her father, she looked at the clear, glittering waters as she plucked a lily from its bed, traced the edges of the petals with her fingers. For a time, they did not speak, only listened to the river's soothing murmurs. Cila glanced at her father.

Fingers playing over the pouch he always carried, Izrak's gaze was fixed on the horizon, as though searching for something only he could find. *No. Waiting for someone who will never return.*

"Papa, are you going to leave us again?"

The dead man's hand closed tight around the pouch; he looked at it for a moment, then placed it inside his tunic. "No, my daughter, I will not leave you again. I promise."

Smiling, Cila took a mushroom from the basket and ate it. She ate another.

Izrak laughed. "Save some for us, little rabbit."

Cila giggled, took one more, and handed it to her father. Izrak hesitated, turning the mushroom over in his fingers. He ate it.

"How does it taste, Papa?"

The dead man stared at her for a moment, shook his head, and chuckled. "Let us return home, little rabbit. Your mother will soon be expecting this fine harvest."

Laughing, Cila leapt to her feet. "Yes, Papa." The girl skipped ahead several paces and turned to face him. "I'll race you! If you catch me before we make it home, you win!"

* * *

That evening, Cila and her mother ate alone. Her father's absence at dinner was expected, but Ryol's absence was unusual, discomforting. Her brother cherished their meals together as much as any family could wish for. *What could make him so mad?* Cila played with her stew as Lebi spoke of Ryol's argument with their father. After her mother had finished, Cila sat quietly for a time.

Cila let go of her spoon. "Where did Ryol go?"

Lebi frowned, peered out the window into the dusky gloom. "I do not know, dear," she said, more to herself, the knuckles of one hand pressed to her lips. "I am sure he will return soon, and in better spirits."

"Where's Papa? Did he go look for him?"

"He…" Lebi paled, drew a hand across her eyes. A moment passed, and she looked at Cila, her lips cracked in a brittle smile. "Your father went to help Bogda bring in his pigs."

Cila scrunched her face at this. "But why won't he go look for Ryol?"

"Your father is just giving him space. Maybe," Lebi turned her gaze to the window once more, "he, too, needs some space." A nervous chuckle broke from her. "You know how hot their tempers can burn…"

Cila stared at the stew before her, studying the bits of sausage, potato, and mushroom, held together by the warm broth, all sheltered within the sturdy bowl. *Why can't we be like that?* Jealousy flared in the girl. All the other girls, the ones who laughed at her, had normal homes, happy families. None seemed to have that cold shadow, that dark cloud, hanging forever over her own home. *I just want our family to be like theirs. Normal. Together. Whole….*

Pushing the bowl away, Cila stood. "Fine. I'll go look for him." Her cheeks were flushed; her breath quickened. She bolted for the door, but Lebi flew from the table to bar her exit.

"No, Cila. I already had one child run off today. I will not have it so with you."

"Then we'll go together!" Cila's eyes reddened, welled with tears.

"No, Cila!" Lebi's lips were pale, drawn tight. Her amber eyes blazed, brooking no reproach.

Crying, Cila turned away. She felt as though the earth trembled beneath her feet, as though the walls of her home were crumbling around her. Stomach roiling, Cila's mind spun, caught in a whirlwind of forces that she did not understand, could not control.

Suddenly, warmth enfolded her as arms closed around her shoulders, infused her with calm. The ground stood still; her mind steadied, came to rest.

Lebi knelt behind her daughter, held Cila in a tight embrace. "I know it is hard right now, dear child." She turned the girl to face her. "I will talk to your father when he returns. But Ryol will come home soon, I am sure. All will be well."

Her mother offered a faint smile. Cila wiped her eyes and nodded her head.

"Now, go wash before bed. I will come read to you before you sleep," Lebi said, rising to her feet.

Cila hugged her mother one last time, then went to do as she was bid.

* * *

A scream dragged Cila from her sleep. Clutching her furs, the girl sat up, body wracked with a shivering born not of the cold. The candle beside her bed had burned out. Only the moon's shallow light trickled in through the window. It did little to stave off the darkness that thickened about her, bubbling up from living shadows growing far beyond their natural limit.

Another scream ripped through the house.

"Mama!" Cila cried into the black. Silence was the only reply.

Then, muffled sounds of struggle seeped through the walls of her room. A faint snarling—a wolf on the hunt—prowled the hallway beyond her door. *Did one of Bogda's dogs get inside?* Cila tossed the fur cover to the ground and crawled beneath her bed. *Just like Ryol told me to do…*

Someone entered the main room. Cila fought to hold her breath against the battering of her heart. *Ryol! Did he come back?* The girl was about to climb out from under the bed when her door burst open. A pair of heavy, muddy boots stomped into the room, the silver gleam of a blade falling into view. Cila jolted the bed as she lurched away from the menacing figure.

"Cila!" the deepening voice cried out.

Ryol! The thought crashed through Cila's mind, propelling her forward. At that same moment, a sickening, gut-wrenching sound seethed from their parents' room. Ryol suddenly fled her room. Unconscious of the action, the girl dug her nails into the wood, clinging to the floor with bloodless fingers... Waiting... Praying...

A moment, a lifetime, passed, and Ryol's shout broke the fugue of Cila's mind. "What have you done? Get away from her!" An infernal roar met her brother's challenge.

Bodies slammed and rolled against the hallway wall. The house itself shook under the impacts as the battle drew closer to Cila's room. The girl wanted desperately to go to her brother, to help him, but the roots of fear sprang from her flesh, reached far and sank deep into the ground to drink of the terror-soaked soil. The rush of blood roared in her ears, curdled in her veins.

Ryol fell in through the doorway. Rolling on a crimson-painted neck, his head turned

towards Cila, listless eyes staring at her as the
sword clattered across the floor, coming to
rest near the bed. That feral snarl stalked just
beyond the door. Ryol's body jerked towards
the door, then was dragged over the threshold.
Those same sickening sounds seethed from the
black once more. Cila quickly reached for the
sword, grabbed it by the blade, and pulled it
towards her.

Pale feet stepped into the room. *Papa?* Tears
welled in her eyes as her grip tightened on the
blade. Izrak moved to the bed, then stood still,
for a heartbeat, for two, for three... Skeletal
fingers wrapped around the edge of the frame.
The wood groaned for an instant, then leapt
from the floor to crash against the wall.

Cila lifted the sword against her father
as she stumbled back towards the window.
The moon's cold light drew her into its silver
embrace, washing the rune-engraved blade in
its argent gleam. Her wounded hands quivered,
and Izrak's sword wept rubrous tears. Chilled
glass pressed against her back, sapping what
little strength remained to a girl whose courage
had been taxed beyond all mercy. Cila slumped
against the panes as the sword fell to her side.

Izrak drew near, his maw drawn in its
sanguinary smile, looming over his daughter as

death's pale shadow. The dead man reached out, his eyes flared orange, pits set with burning coals....

VIII

A BLADE REBORN

Sight returned to the dead man.

Lying upon a bed of lilies, his gaze was met by the somnolent eye of the moon drifting towards the west. Stars flickered as candles in the quilt of night, beacons guiding the weary moon to its diurnal repose. Envy had flared within Izrak's mind, now replaced by cool sympathy. The moon's journey was not yet over, and many long hours remained until its passing.

An echo, a thought, a memory called to the dead man from the ether. Izrak clutched the worn pouch at his hip. *Please... let me stay. Let me rest here... a little longer.* A task, a purpose, a promise grasped him by the hands. *Cila...* And the dead man rose to his feet.

Standing upon the shore of the dreaming lake, Izrak cast his gaze out over the tranquil waters. The surface of the water was glass, a vast plane of black jade reflecting a dull, silver gleam. With fingers yet closed around the pouch, he took a step towards that frosted void.

Where are you?

"I am here, father," the voice came, a tinkling of bells, as gentle waves rippled out from a dim point of brumal light deep below, "Where you left me." The point of light expanded, growing ever more intense as it climbed towards the surface.

Izrak's grip on the pouch loosened as a cloud of coruscant luminescence emerged from the lake, then coalesced into a blinding flash, dimmed, and began to take form as a delicate figure stepped onto the pulsing waters.

A girl—*no, a woman*—stood before Izrak. Golden locks enwreathed a porcelain face, and eyes of emerald dawn peered into the empty pits of his own. High cheeks flanked a thin nose, set atop a long, slender neck. She was clothed in a flowing gown of glittering starlight. The woman's smile was wistful, the corners of her lips heavy, as though weighed down by a wisdom that is born only of sorrow and understanding. *Just as her mother used to smile… at me…* Though aged ten summers, she was wholly the image of the daughter lost to time and haunted memory.

"What you have done, father, cannot be undone. You must accept this," Cila said, her spectral form hovering just above the water, hair and gown billowing on ethereal winds. "You cannot save her."

Izrak looked away.

"Not as you are."

The dead man turned his dark gaze upon the shade.

"You carry an evil of the old world, an abomination that will lead you only to temptation. To destruction." Cila closed her eyes, a soft smile gracing her lips. "Can you let her go?"

Witch-fire smoldered in the pits of his eyes. Izrak ensnared the pouch at his side. "I... No..." He tore down the hood of his cloak, pressed his fingers against his skull. "No! I cannot!"

Her smile faded, and Cila glared at the dead man. "You must."

A soulless groan fumed from Izrak as he dropped to his knee. "I promised."

Black clouds thundered into the valley, the earth shaking under salvos of concussive force as golden spears of lightning lanced through

the darkling sky. The windmill squealed as
wrathful gusts tore at its battered sails, ground
its rusted hub, and the waters roiled beyond
the spirit, whipped into a primal fury.

"It was a false promise. You were bound by
chains of perversion and darkness." Cila's voice
clapped as the thunder above. "You are a slave!"

Hellfire blazed in the dead man's eyes.
"What choice did I have? Were we meant to
allow evil to prevail?" Izrak's quivering fingers
squeezed the pouch, its charnel contents
clattering together.

"No, father, you were not. But you traded
one evil for another, and in so doing, you *all*
lost your way." The fiery spirit held out her
hand. "The path is not closed to you," she said,
and the fires dimmed in Izrak's eyes. "Free
yourself. You know the way. You have always
known."

The dead man stood, ripped the pouch
from his belt, and with faltering steps,
shambled into the waters. Tendrils of sickly
green ghost-light burst from the pouch, coiling
around his limbs, his neck. Serpents of Hell,
the coils constricted, dragging Izrak to his
knees. Frothing waves lashed at his waist as he
was dragged lower still. Fire blazed anew in
his abyssal pits as he clawed at those wicked
energies—those eternal chains.

"I was meant to serve one greater than you," he growled, struggling against the revenant serpents. His roar challenged the thunder for supremacy. Izrak began to rise, but quickly subdued, was forced back down, his head just above the surface. The fires in his eyes flickered out. His body calmed. *Not by my own power...* "No more," the dead man whispered, and allowed himself to be pulled under.

Izrak surged from the depths, his chains broken.

Cila began to sink into the calming waters as her father stumbled towards her. "Let her go," she said, hand outstretched. "Leave her in the past."

Glancing at his pouch one final time, remembering whose malevolence it held, Izrak placed it in Cila's hand, pressed it to her palm. He knelt as the spirit sank lower, still holding her hand.

Crystal waters caressed her cheeks as Cila gazed at him. "At last, I see you as you were," came her voice, dreaming, as her eyes closed, "in those summers long past..." And she drifted into the depths.

Izrak doubled over on the shore. His eyes widened as he gazed upon the glassy reflection resting on the water's surface. The image of a man returned his stare. With flaxen hair falling in lazy waves to his shoulders, and eyes of jade peering over high cheeks and a broad nose, Izrak lifted his free hand to his face, traced a clean-shaven jaw, and felt the fingertips brush over flesh.

A faint smile touched his lips. *I knew you, once…* The image flickered, began to fade. *For centuries, I sought to bring you back.* He pulled his lips taut, closed his eyes. *I tried. So many times…* Izrak looked upon his reflection. *Yet that was another time, another life. I cannot change what I have done. The dark powers cannot forgive, cannot redeem. Evil offers no respite, only…* A faint azure gleam kindled in his eyes.

The image of the man vanished, and the face of death smiled at him once more.

A sudden weight materialized in his grip.

Izrak stood, drawing a sword from the deep.

The rune-engraved blade was broad, razor-edged—unbreakable. *I knew you, once… in another time, another life.* Thunder cracked, and the blade's runes gleamed gold under the lightning as it streaked across the sky. The warrior ran his fingers over the inscriptions. *Mercy… Vengeance… My father's sword.*

"Spazislova—The Word of the Redeemer."
He pressed the hilt to his brow. *A blade reborn
ought to bear a new name, a new purpose; the
Redeemer spoke His Word, and the people of this
land heeded it not. He offered His mercy, and
being rejected, promised a time of retribution, of
vengeance.* "A new purpose. A new name."

A memory swelled within Izrak's mind; a
morning on the riverbank, he and his daughter
sat watching the swift waters course as blood
through the veins of a land returning to life.
She asked about her name, what it meant; *Cila,*
he said, *is a word from the old tongue; perhaps an
odd name for a girl,* he confessed, *but one that
has proved true all the same.*

The cold blaze of cerulean fire ignited in
the hollows of his eyes. Izrak's grip on the hilt
tightened as he looked upon the gleaming
blade. *Cila.* The warrior uttered a single word
as he thrust the sword skyward: "Power."

A bolt of golden lightning cleaved the
heavens, plummeting in a crackling arc,
crashing upon the blade, surging over its
gleaming edges. Izrak's body quaked under
the force of the strike. A moment, a lifetime,
passed. And another began. Energy crawled
on spider legs over the blade as the warrior's
cerulean glare burned furiously. He swung the
blade down in a resplendent arc; that same

instant, a fusillade of thunderclaps hammered the valley, and a wave of pressure rolled over the lake, no longer dreaming.

And the darkness covering the land of Enostran trembled…

Imperceptible to all, but Izrak Laav.

IX

OLD WAYS

Unbound by wanton hunger, by false promise, the warrior stood upon the blooming shore. Lilies danced about his boots, their pearlescent petals shivering under the ringing hum of Cila's might as shadows retreated from the shore, fleeing over the clearing to cower within the dark refuge of the forest. Izrak ran his hand along the length of the blade.

For centuries, his mind had been broken, lost in a black labyrinth of uncertainty, of fear, of rage. Shackled with hatred, driven by the lash of his faceless masters, he had wandered Enostran with perverse intent and an empty hope.

No more… Izrak pressed the blade to his brow. He sensed Cila's thirst for retribution pulsing, quivering through the blade like an arrow set to a drawn bowstring. The mist surrounding the lake cleared, revealing a great temple looming over the far shore. A wan figure, clothed in muddied white, flitted across the shore towards the ancient structure.

A new purpose…

"Elishei. I will not abandon you."

The lilies ceased their dance. Izrak saw their petals reaching like fingers towards a point behind him. The warrior spun about with sword raised. Several paces away, the forest spirit stood, a hand pressed to his side, the leaves of his crown rustling in the brittle breeze.

Izrak leveled the point of his blade at the spirit. "I am through with you, Old One. Stand aside, or I will destroy you."

The spirit seemed to look past him. "You already have…" he said, as if to himself.

Izrak tilted his head, lowered his sword.

"I told you to leave, warrior, that you interfered in matters that did not concern you. Those of the living." The spirit stepped forward, lifting an accusing finger. "For you are an abomination, born of fear and faithlessness. Blind with hunger and rage, you have led them here, brought death to the girl."

"Led whom here?" Izrak said, peering left, then right, into the woods.

"I no longer possess the strength to fight them…" The spirit's gnarled fingers clutched the robes of moss at his side.

"Your only concern should lie with me, Old One."

The spirit chuckled, like the popping of branches. "And so, it does." His gaze bore into Izrak. "What is it you seek, warrior? You cannot erase your crimes. There is no going back."

Izrak stepped closer. "No, there is not."

Shifting his gaze, the spirit peered at the gleaming sword. "Perhaps," he looked at Izrak, "you may yet find what you seek." Lifting his head to the sky, the spirit let his hand fall from his side. Amber tears of sap seeped from a deep, penetrating wound.

Izrak stared at the wound, then glanced at his sword. "It seems my search will be a long one."

"Such is the path you have chosen."

The warrior sheathed his blade. "What is your name?"

"I have many names. Every tree of the forest bears my signature, as numerous as the stars above," the spirit said, sweeping a hand over the valley. "Yet you may call me Shuvo, as I am called by the people of this land."

Looking away, Izrak was quiet for a time. He plucked a lily from its bed. "What will happen to the forest?"

Shuvo smiled. "I do not know. Like any young bird that leaves the nest, it must learn to fend for itself."

The warrior remained silent, tracing the petals with his finger.

"Come. We must leave. They draw near."

"Who?" Izrak placed the flower in his satchel and moved towards the spirit. "What else hunts the girl?"

"Demons...."

Shuvo lifted his hands, palms turned upwards. "I will do what I may to obscure the path." Mists rose to surround the lake once more, shrouding the far side in a gray haze. "I shall go on ahead, that the child be not alone." The spirit's body burst into a howling column of air, rising into the night. "Follow, swiftly, to the temple." His voice flowed back in waves over the waters. "And pray to your god, your Redeemer, that they do not find us."

The warrior shot off like an arrow into the

mists. Izrak's hand tightened on the grip of his sword. *No, Shuvo.* Cila thrummed with furious anticipation. *It is they who must pray.*

* * *

Trust is a double-edged sword. In untrained, careless hands, trust becomes as dangerous to one as to the other. Often, one attacks when they should defend, parries, and ripostes, when they should bind and cross over. Trust demands years of practice and a firm grip by both hands, that it may be relied upon for protection and safety.

Unlike a sword, however, how one trains to trust is not clear; there are no manuals from which to practice the forms, no instructors with which to hone techniques. As with love, only hard-won experience, and countless wounds, can teach. And like love, with courage and faith, one may learn to trust.

Such were the thoughts of Izrak Laav as he emerged from the woods and stepped into a large glade, a natural courtyard laid out before the lakeside fane.

Cyclopean slabs of cracked stone, fifteen feet in height, as old as the earth itself, were arrayed in a circle around a massive oak whose age counted millennia. Standing at two hundred feet, the thick branches and spiraling boughs formed a canopy of verdant dusk; giant acorns hung within the boughs, emanating a soft, golden light. Even one such as Izrak marveled at the beauty of the scene as he stepped between the stone sentinels.

A stone altar, darkened red by countless sacrifices, stood at the base of the trunk. A bed of moss and leaves lay atop the altar, and lying upon the bed was Elishei, eyes closed, breathing faintly.

A flash of steel, and Izrak's sword was in his hand. He rushed to the girl's side, reaching out to her. *What is this?*

"Fear not, warrior. The girl sleeps." A current of air flowed down from the boughs, and from a swirling mass of leaves Shuvo materialized near the altar. "Not a drop of virgin's blood has wet this stone in five-hundred summers."

Cerulean flamed in the warrior's eyes. "And it will be five hundred more before I see this child sacrificed! You will not have her life to save your own."

A shiver ran through the eldritch oak. Shuvo stepped forward, hands uplifted. "You must not take—"

"Enough, Shuvo." Izrak's voice was a grinding of stone. "You may spend whatever time you have left in peace, but if you continue to stand in my way, I will end you now."

Elishei stirred, rolled to her side.

Shuvo glanced at the girl. "Izrak Laav, you must listen to me."

"I am taking Elishei home."

"No!" The terrified shriek came from atop the altar. Izrak whirled to face it. Elishei sat huddled, knees pulled into her chest, a trembling hand pointing behind him. "Don't let them take me! Not again."

Branches snapped as long nails raked over stone. Izrak spun about to find Matvan, Vasi, and Resh, shirtless with trousers in tatters, standing before the temple slabs.

"What?" He glanced at Shuvo, then at the haggard men. "What are you doing here? I told you to go back. It is not safe."

Resh's eyes glittered darkly as he drew his fingers over the gashes in his chest. "No, it isn't."

Vasi stepped forward, his red hair bristling, lips drawn back in a ravenous grin. "There you are, little rabbit. Oh, how much trouble you've caused us…" He looked at Matvan and groaned. "Let me take a bite. Just one."

For a moment, the older man stood silent, chest heaving, the veins of his neck bulging, writhing like worms. "Orved wants her back. Unharmed… Whole."

A guttural snarl rumbled from Vasi's throat. "To the devil with Orved. All he feeds us is rotten scraps! I want something fresh." He leered at Elishei, drool spilling from quivering lips. "I want her."

Throwing off his cloak and satchel, Izrak sidestepped in front of Elishei and dropped into a low stance.

Vasi snorted. "That won't save you. Not from me." A quivering tremor shot through his body. He lurched forwards, bones cracking and reforming, as he sank into a bestial crouch. "No mortal weapon can!" Vasi snarled and slammed his fists into the earth as a coat of blood-red fur erupted from his flesh. He leapt to his feet as his arms extended, elongated fingers ending in black claws long as knives; his lips peeled back to reveal a muzzle of jagged fangs; yellow eyes shimmered in the faded glow of the oak's seeds.

The monster's laughter pitched to a blood-chilling howl.

"I'll pick my teeth with it," he growled, lips contorting in a mockery of human speech, "when I'm done with her."

Vasi's charge was a rubrous blur. Izrak narrowly ducked his sweeping claws, their tips tearing the leather cap from his head. The warrior shot upwards, Cila rising in a silver arc as the blade's edge carved a crimson path through Vasi's chest.

The demon leapt back, groping at the wound. His hand came away slick with blood. Panting, his baleful glare snapped back at Izrak. A feral roar exploded from Vasi as he charged with renewed fury.

Izrak met the demon's assault with a thrust. But Vasi sidestepped the warrior's blade, batting it aside. Razor claws raked through Izrak's mail as he leapt away. Before he could recover, a blow slammed into his chest, sending him crashing against the oak's great trunk. Dozens of fist-sized seeds plummeted from the shaken boughs, each landing with a dull thud as Izrak fell to the ground.

Dazed, Izrak clutched at the trunk, struggling to rise. A girl's scream ripped through the turbid silence of the fane. He looked towards the altar. Vasi stood before the blood-drunk stone, lifted a flailing Elishei. The demon's maw seethed with slaver as he drew in his prey. Azure fire blazed in Izrak's eyes; the warrior was on his feet in an instant.

A bolt of shadow, Izrak lunged at the demon, sword held overhead; he swung. Cila struck like lightning as the warrior cleaved through Vasi's forearms. Elishei fell to the ground alongside the severed limbs. Vasi staggered backwards, howling in agony as dark blood poured from the gaping wounds at his elbows.

"Resh!" Matvan shouted as he metamorphosed into a sable lupine monstrosity.

Resh howled, sprang forwards as golden fur spread over his form, fangs dripping as he and Matvan raced towards the wailing Vasi.

At that same instant, Shuvo dug his fingers into the soil. The wooden cords of his arms rippled, writhed, and tendrils of iron-hard roots and vines burst from the ground beneath Matvan and Resh, slithering about their limbs, constricting, pulling them down into the dirt.

Amber lifeblood spilled from Shuvo's wound, and the roots and vines began to wither, barely withstanding the beasts raging against their verdant cage.

Near the altar, a wrathful Vasi trembled in pain, and with a desperate howl, made a final lunge for Elishei.

Izrak stepped in, driving Cila's blade, between shattered teeth, through the monster's quivering maw. Vasi's yellow eyes fixed upon the warrior as his body shuddered with violent spasms, then glazed over and rolled back into his skull. The beast's corpse fell to its knees, and Izrak pulled the blade free as it slumped to the ground.

The massive bole of the oak groaned under unseen strain. Shuvo stood, stumbled back.

Elishei scrambled over to the spirit.

The roots and vines entrapping Matvan and Resh began to fall away, and the monsters tore themselves free from their grasp. They crawled from the earth like demons out of Hell. Barking ferociously, they assailed the warrior.

A whirlwind of death surged across the temple grounds. Izrak danced through a haze of slashing claws and snapping fangs. Cila's song gave rhythm to the warrior's strikes as her edge whistled through the air. Dark blood drizzled over Izrak's shredded armor as he rained cut after cut upon those abominations. Yet, the fury of their attacks only grew with each wound the warrior inflicted.

The winds shifted, and Izrak was driven back under a flurry of savage swipes that rent his pallid flesh.

Izrak staggered, and in a mad rush, the demonic pair charged the warrior, forcing him to the ground. Matvan wrenched Cila from Izrak's grip, tossing it aside, where it clattered on the ground next to Elishei. Resh's fangs sank into Izrak's shoulder as Matvan's claws closed around his skull. Rending, crushing, their blasphemous strength strained the limits of his preternatural durability. Cerulean flashed in the pits of his eyes as he roared.

Gripping Matvan's neck with his free hand, Izrak yanked down and smashed his head into the demon's muzzle. Matvan reeled, and the warrior drove an armored knee into the sable beast's chest, sending him sprawling. That same instant, he pummeled Resh's golden head with an iron fist, turning his near eye to pulp before the monster rolled away, whining. Izrak quickly fell upon Resh, locking his skeletal fingers around the demon's throat.

Suddenly, Matvan seized him, dragging Izrak away from Resh. Resh was still coughing, gasping for breath as Matvan's jaws closed around Izrak's skull. Something cracked against the beast's head. Matvan snorted, released him.

Izrak looked towards Elishei. The girl snatched another giant seed from the ground and hurled it at Matvan, this time striking him on the nose. Matvan whined, closed his eyes in reflex.

Rising, Izrak sent his fist crashing into Matvan's jaw, shattering fangs and bones. The beast staggered back a step, two, and the warrior tackled him. Izrak pummeled the demon's head with a hail of blows, then tore into Matvan's throat with his teeth.

"Warrior!" came Elishei's cry.

Eyes blazing, Izrak looked at the girl, his crimson teeth dripping gore. Elishei held Cila in trembling hands. *Am I no different?* His eyes dimmed. *No more… I am a monster no more!* Izrak jumped to his feet.

Elishei threw the sword. "Catch!"

Wheezing, whimpering, Matvan rolled over, trying to crawl away.

Izrak caught his sword and in a single motion, buried Cila's blade through Matvan's heart. The monster's claws raked impotently at the soil, then settled into deathly calm.

Even as the warrior ended Matvan's wrath, Resh recovered and charged Elishei. Shuvo lunged into his path. With a bark, Resh clamped his jaws on the spirit's shoulder, twisted, and hurled Shuvo towards the trunk of the oak, tearing his arm from his body. Resh bit down, and Shuvo's arm splintered between his teeth. His feral gaze snapped back to Elishei.

"No!" Izrak shot towards the beast. He was too slow. Resh held the girl close, a single, long claw caressing Elishei's pale throat.

Hackles bristling, Resh growled. "Throw down your sword, grave-spawn! She goes with me. Or…" He pressed the point into her flesh. Drops of crimson rilled down her neck.

Grip tightening on Cila's hilt, Izrak snarled and stepped forward.

Resh, his ears tucked back, pressed his claws to Elishei's chest. "I'll tear her apart in front of you!"

Izrak halted, his eyes smoldering. He looked upon the runes of Cila's blade, repeated their inscriptions like a chant in his mind: *Mercy… Vengeance… Mercy… Vengeance…* Shuvo was leaning against the ancient oak, staring back at him. His wound had stopped bleeding; the flow of amber reduced to a trickle.

Izrak turned his blade down and drove it into the earth. He took a step back.

Winds began to flow over the temple grounds. Shuvo chanted in low tones carried on the sighing currents, mingled with the soughing of the boughs in the vast canopy overhead. The pale light of the glowing seeds flickered, brightened as Shuvo's body dissembled and merged with the oak.

Black clouds of mist gathered about the temple's cyclopean stones, rising to obscure the moon's glow, and shrouding all beyond the light of the oak in unnatural darkness.

"What is this?" Resh said. He tightened his hold on Elishei.

The shrieking winds were the only reply.

Shuvo's voice came to Izrak as a whisper in his mind. *My time is over. I can give you one chance. Are you ready?*

The warrior's gaze was fixed on the demon. *I am.*

The light of the seeds flared brilliant white for an instant, then absolute darkness descended upon the temple grounds. Even Resh's lupine eyes were blind to all around him.

Izrak's undead sight was unhindered.

He watched as the beast looked about with furtive glances, huffing the air. Resh growled,

backed away towards the altar. Silently, the
warrior pulled his sword from the ground.

Resh stumbled into the altar and lost his
hold on Elishei. The girl slipped under his arm
and scurried away. He lurched towards her. "I
smell you. You can't—" But he never finished.

Izrak flew through the shadows—death's
swift messenger—a dirge singing on Cila's
edge as the blade split apart Resh's skull. Izrak
tore the blade free. The demon's corpse fell
twitching upon the altar, a final sacrifice to the
passing of old gods—and old ways.

X

THREADBARE

Cold light spilled into the clearing beneath the oak as the black mists lifted from the stones surrounding the temple. Slowly, the mists expanded, thinning as they drifted towards the canopy. A gust of wind sighed through the leaves, and borne away upon night's last breath, the disembodied vapors dissipated into the gray of approaching dawn.

Elishei huddled against the ages-old tree. She faced away from the altar, weeping into her arms.

Izrak looked upon her for a moment. *He can no longer hear you, child.* His hand drifted towards his belt. *Why do we cling so tightly to the dead?* The warrior's fingers closed around what was no longer there. *No. Not the dead.* His hand moved to his sword, grasped Cila's hilt in a tight embrace. *We cling to the memory of life. It is there that we find our power.*

Lifting his cloak and satchel from the grass, Izrak approached the girl with apprehensive steps. "Elishei."

The weeping ceased. Her form went rigid.

"Are you hurt?"

Elishei pressed her shivering body against the oak, said nothing.

"We must leave. This is no place for you to linger."

Elishei peered over her shoulder at the corpse upon the altar, then at Izrak.

"Those monsters can no longer hurt you, child."

Eyes wide, Elishei shrank away. With a tremulous voice, she asked, "What about you?"

Izrak was silent as he threw on his cloak, its thick canvas spilling over the tattered remains of his armor. The warrior glanced back over his shoulder at the savaged remains of his lupine foes.

"Matvan claimed to be your father. He—"

Elishei shot to her feet, facing him. Her cheeks were flushed, her fists clenched. "That monster was not my father!"

"No, Elishei, of course not." Izrak moved closer. Elishei flinched, her eyes darting to the warrior's sword. Cila pulsed with gentle force. Izrak drew the sword slowly and thrust it into the ground. He took another step. "Who were they? Why did those demons hunt you?"

"It doesn't matter anymore. Shuvo was going to help me. Help us." Tears returned to her eyes. "Now he's gone," she said, voice weak on her lips. "I don't have anywhere to go."

"You are from Novogor, are you not?" Izrak said, holding out his hand. "Come. I will take you to your parents."

"I'm from Ryaz." Elishei sniffled and wiped her nose on the back of her hand. "My parents are dead."

"Forgive me, child." Izrak lowered his hand. "Do you have no other family?"

"Just my brother."

"Where is he?"

Elishei blanched. "*He* has him. The sorcerer…" Her breath now came in rapid bursts. "I need to go!" She stumbled forward, stopped, swayed, holding her head. Her voice was frail. "I need to save Grigor…" Elishei took another faltering step.

"Elishei, wait. You must calm yourself."

"I… need to… the others…"

Izrak reached out, caught the girl as she nearly fainted. She breathed deep, steadying herself against him. "Elishei, do not fear me." Her grip tightened on him. "I mean only to help you." She nodded her head against his chest. Holding Elishei's shoulders, he stepped back. "Now, tell me what happened. Where is your brother?"

Elishei wiped her eyes with pallid hands. "They took us from Ryaz and sold us to the sorcerer. He still has my brother."

"A sorcerer? In Novogor?"

"Yes. They called him Orved."

Izrak stared for a moment, then shook his head.

"They took us to an old castle in the city. He kept us in the dungeons. There were others, too. Other children. Sometimes, they took one of them. We never saw them again. But the chanting. And the screams," the blood drained from her face, "the screams never stopped…" Elishei's voice trailed off as her body shivered.

Izrak knelt before her. "I will not let them take you again. Now tell me, how did you escape?"

"A friend." Elishei calmed, the color returning to her face. "One of the sorcerer's... men, Gromm. He helped me. Said it was all he could do. He told me to find help. But those monsters found me in the city. They chased me into the forest, and—"

"You chanced upon me."

"Shuvo found me after I ran from you. He told me not to trust you. That you were one of them." Elishei bit her bottom lip and looked away. "He swore to protect me."

"I see…" Izrak stood. The warrior looked to the east, saw pale gold light creeping tentatively into the temple grounds as the sun's crown peeked over the eastern hills. "Do you trust me?"

Hazel eyes sparkling greenly in the light of dawn, Elishei peered into the warrior's hollow eyes. "I don't know," she said after a moment. "Doesn't seem like I have a choice."

"You always have a choice." Izrak reached into his satchel. He withdrew the lily, held it out to her. "Yet, you would be wise to trust me now."

Elishei reached out, hesitated, then took the flower. "It's beautiful. But why?"

"It was her favorite."

"Who's?"

Izrak faced the east, his hand resting upon Cila's pommel. "Come. I will bring you to Ryaz. I will return to help your brother once I know you are safe."

Elishei circled in front of him. "I'm not leaving without Grigor! I'm going with you. Besides, I can help."

"No. I promised to protect you. I cannot risk Orved capturing you again."

The girl started to turn. "I'm not leaving without my brother."

"Wait." Izrak took her hand.

"Let go of me!"

Izrak held on as Elishei tried desperately to pull away. "At least let me take you back to the church. You can wait for me there."

"No!" Elishei faced him, face flushed, chest heaving. "You want me to trust you? Let me go. I can help you. Just like before," she said, pointing to Matvan's sable corpse.

Izrak let go of her hand. He looked at the blood-soaked carcass. Cila thrummed at his side. "So be it. But you will stay at my side and do exactly as I command. Agreed?"

The girl nodded. A shadow of a smile touched her lips as she set the lily in her hair.

"Very well." Izrak turned towards the lake. "Let us leave this place. I must tend to my armor. You must wash and rest."

"But we—"

"Must be prepared and rested. You will need your strength, child. Your journey is far from over," the warrior said as he guided Elishei towards the lake. "And I fear my battle has only just begun."

* * *

Elishei stirred as she lay in fitful sleep beneath an ancient pine. Her fingers sank into the shade-dappled bed of needles upon which she slept; a wan cry passed her lips, fleeing some strange, new nightmare that tormented her repose. Or perhaps, it was an old, familiar nightmare; that stalks one through alleys of dusk; that hunts one through forests of night-veiled terror; that lurks under one's bed whispering portents of doom—the nightmare that stands over one waking with a mirthless smile and eyes of dread promise.

Izrak crouched, pulled his cloak up over the girl's shoulders. *A small comfort, for one so haunted.* Elishei's fingers relaxed as the trembling of her body ceased. *A little comfort was all she ever asked.* Elishei drew the cloak tight and, after a moment, her breathing calmed. Izrak piled a handful of wild berries and a pair of apples he had gathered beside her.

Izrak rose, then approached the diamond-studded waters glistening in the pale gold of early morning. Long blades of green grass damp with dew lapped against his boots as he came upon a fallen log near the shoreline.

He unhooked Cila from his belt, placed the sword against it. After setting his belt and satchel on the log, he doffed his jerkin. Naught remained but soiled leather strips held together by threads. Izrak salvaged the largest pieces to be washed and used as wrappings for Elishei's battered feet. Setting the leather aside, the warrior then removed his armor, laid the chain mail out before him. The mail had fared but little better, yet the sleeves remained mostly intact. Izrak would use those to repair the gashes in the torso. But first, the mail needed to be washed. Reaching into his satchel, he withdrew pliers, a hide pouch containing spare rings, and a cloth rag. Izrak knelt by the cool water, soaked the cloth, and wrung it out.

The warrior heard a raven's caw, the flutter of wings; for an instant, all sound and light faded, dimmed, as though the world had plunged into frigid depths, only to rise gasping to the surface. A troubled sigh passed between his teeth.

Izrak rose, turned to greet his visitor.

Olesia stood beside the dreaming girl. The Omen glanced down at Elishei, then back at the warrior; her stormy eyes drowned in a sadness that did not belong to her. Olesia lifted her hands from beneath her cloak and signed: *She looks so much like her.*

"Yes," Izrak said as he returned to his equipment. He sat, ran the cloth over his blood-encrusted mail.

The Omen stepped silently to Izrak and sat before him. *Is that why?*

"I could not leave her."

No. You never could, Izrak Laav. Olesia's gaze passed over the unadorned belt, bereft of the worn pouch that had clung to it for so long. *Where is Kalis?*

"Where she belongs…"

Izrak hung the bloody cloth over the log, gathered the pliers and spare rings, and set to repairing his mail.

Olesia climbed to her knees and unclasped her cloak, letting it fall into a black pool about her. The black silk of her blouse shimmered in the sunlight beneath a dusk-gray sarafan trimmed in black lace and embroidered with eldritch patterns, which served purposes other than decorative. From her satchel Olesia drew a roll of dark leather. She spread open the roll before her; inside were scissors, several straight and curved suturing needles of various lengths, and a spool of tenebrous thread that looked as though it were spun from the very fabric of the Void.

The Omen took a small, curved needle in one hand and pressed the point to her fingertip. A crimson teardrop welled about the tip of the needle, then rolled up along its length until the needle was coated in blood. The blood dissolved, as if absorbed; the needle flashed pale green, then returned to its natural dull metallic sheen.

As Izrak finished his work—what little he could do—Olesia threaded the witch needle with the darkling thread. *Her own hair… Is there nothing they will not take from us?* Olesia's hand fell on his arm. The warrior looked up from his work. She was smiling.

Rise, Izrak Laav. It is your body that now needs mending. The ritual will take time, for the wounds you have suffered are many. Tell me your tale. Tell me how you came to be protector of this girl…

Izrak was still as he finished his tale, while the Omen finished her final suture.

The warrior said nothing as Olesia packed her tools away. Whatever effect his tale had had on her remained a mystery. Still, he could not escape the feeling that she understood more than mere appearances suggested. Izrak gathered up her cloak and stepped towards her. Olesia turned so that her back faced him. Placing the cloak over her shoulders, Izrak fastened the clasp. As he did, Olesia leaned back, letting her weight rest against him. His hands lingered on Olesia's shoulders for a heartbeat, for two, for three, then slid down her arms as he held her.

After a moment, Olesia faced him. Tears shimmering with faint hues of green, yellow, and pink—an aurora spilling out over oceans of pale night—rolled down her cheeks. *You do not know what it is you set out to do. Not truly.*

"Zheso's fate is no longer my concern," Izrak said, wiping the tears from her cheeks. "Let our masters send their assassins. I will sow the earth with their bones. I am no longer a tool… no longer a slave."

Death at the hands of your own would be a mercy… Head lowered, the Omen backed away. *You have changed, Izrak Laav, it is true. You have regained a power once lost to you.* Hope bloomed in her face, fleeting, then wilted into despair. *Yet even with your sword, it may not be enough. I do not know what Orved wants with Elishei. But I know what horrors await you if you challenge him, for his powers are beyond even you, Ferryman. I know that he is one of the masters. Orved Sepah is one of the High Priests.*

Azure rage flashed in the pits of Izrak's eyes. Cila's blade rattled in its scabbard. "How long have you known?"

Olesia looked away. *I learned of his identity soon after my voice was taken.*

"Why did you not tell me?"

I was afraid of what you might do if you knew the truth. I was afraid of what else they might take from me… I was afraid that I would lose you.

Cila's trembling ceased as the fires dimmed in the warrior's eyes.

"This is not the world we fought for. This is not the world we sought to build. High Priest or no, Orved's evil cannot be allowed to endure. I will not abandon Elishei and Grigor, the other children." Izrak held Olesia's head in his hands. "Nor will I abandon you."

* * *

The sun was approaching its peak when Elishei woke. She rubbed the sleep from her eyes, blinked, and found a gathering of apples and berries. Her mouth watered as her stomach growled; the girl grinned wolfishly. It had been almost two days since she had last eaten. Elishei's face pinched at the memory of the slop fed to her in the sorcerer's dungeon. Seizing an apple, she devoured the fruit in seconds, shoved a fistful of the berries into her mouth with no care given to the good manners her mother had spent years trying to teach her.

A pit formed in her stomach as a warm tear trickled down her cheek. Elishei wiped it away, ate a few more berries—one at a time.

She paused, furrowed her brow, as she was about to eat the last apple. *Did the dead man gather these for me?* Elishei peered through the skirt of pine boughs hanging about her. *Where is he?*

Taking the apple, Elishei wrapped the cloak around her shoulders and slipped out from under the tree. The dead man was not difficult to find.

There—she saw him seated on a log near the shore, laying strips of leather over the bark. He was not wearing his armor. Her eyes widened at the sight. Elishei might have assumed, even expected, to find a skeleton.

Instead, she saw a body, with flesh and
thew—though his flesh was pale, withered,
and stretched over muscles that looked dried
and hard as ironwood—like that of a normal
man. Taking a few steps closer, she noticed that
the dead man's flesh was webbed with black
stitching, as if he were an old doll held together
by threads. *There are so many…* A shiver laced
her spine with black threads of its own.

After a few deep breaths, the girl moved
towards him. As she drew near, Elishei heard
the dead man singing—verse intoned on
death's whisper from an age forgotten:

There, upon the cold shores of Akheron
The Ferryman broods and suffers and waits,
For some poor soul to cross his haunted path
Which he travels endless; this is his fate.

And to cross his path, means swift and sure death,
Even as the pale River ceaseless flows,
For his tread is ghostly, blade hissing breath
Look not, you shan't see him! Death's pale shadow.

Flee if you dare, but know the price is paid,
For a soul, led from blood and broken bone;
And rich with burnished coins, dread mien inlaid
He ponders, who'll be left to lead his own.

Elishei stepped beside him. "Who's the Ferryman?"

The dead man was quiet for a moment. "A myth..." He stood, faced her. "How are you, child?" His gaze flicked to the apple. "Did you eat?"

"Yes." Elishei's eyes lingered on the eyeless pits of his skull. It was hard not to stare, not to get lost in that hollow gaze. *How can he see? What does he see?* Prickling warmth flooded her cheeks. She held out the apple. "I saved this for you. Do you still... eat?"

"Not anymore..." With a soft laugh, the dead man sat on the log and gestured in front of him. "Lay down the cloak. Sit and eat your apple while I wrap your feet," he said, nodding to the leather strips.

Elishei sat as she was bid. As the girl ate, she was surprised at the dexterity of his skeletal fingers, possessed by a gentleness that bordered on the ethereal. But she also sensed old wisdom and a dread power contained within those hands. She had not forgotten what his fists had done to the monsters. And what they had done for her.

"I'm sorry, warrior," Elishei said as he finished binding her footwraps. "I never thanked you for what you did. For saving me. I haven't even asked your name..."

Tying the last knot, he looked at her. "I am called Izrak Laav." He stood, offered his hand. She took it, and Izrak helped her to her feet. "And you are welcome."

Standing quietly, wrapped in the cloak, Elishei watched as Izrak donned his mail and fastened his sword belt around his waist. *Right.* She removed the cloak, held it out to the warrior. "Here."

Izrak shook his head. "Keep it, child. The chill of spring is still in the air. And a girl should not go about in a threadbare gown."

Elishei blushed, giggled. "Do you feel it? The cold?"

"I do not. Yet I still remember the way it feels. A phantom chill… We undead are haunted by the memories of past sensation."

"You mean like looking at a painting—of a river—you can hear the water, smell the tall grass on the banks."

"Just so," Izrak said as he placed his satchel over his shoulder. The rings of his mail clinked as it slid into place at his side.

Elishei smiled, then asked, "Why do you wear armor?"

"For the same reason as any warrior," Izrak said as he took his gloves from his satchel and pulled them over his hands. "And because even the dead wish to hide their scars…"

Elishei touched the lily nestled in her hair. "Izrak, who is Cila?"

Izrak turned away, his hand resting on his sword. "She was my daughter…" Without looking back, the warrior moved towards the forest. "Come, child. We must go."

XI

DEATH'S PASSAGE

Elishei followed Izrak through the forest, skirting the edge of the lake. For long hours, the warrior did not speak, but moved with the steady, silent march of inescapable time. They stopped for a short rest after reaching the opposite shore. As Elishei let her feet soak in the water, sipping some of it from her hands, she watched Izrak. Still, he said nothing, standing motionless among the lilies, staring out over the lake. Then, without a word, they traveled on. Shadows lengthened, and the red-tinged sun settled towards the horizon, as Elishei and her deathless guardian once again came to the Old City.

Izrak wanted to go around, but Elishei insisted they go through. It would be faster, she argued, and told him that Shuvo had shown her a quick path through the city. Izrak remained wary of the idea. With his strength and demon-killing sword, Elishei did not understand what gave the warrior pause. She assured him that all would be well, that she felt safe with him.

At last, the warrior relented. And as the sun peeked through the curtain of the western hills, they passed into the city.

Staying close behind the warrior, Elishei guided them through the dark, labyrinthine streets. Sword drawn, Izrak listened long before crossing dusk-veiled alleys, casting furtive glances around every corner. At one such crossing, near the city's edge, the warrior peered into the shadows of an alley. Elishei peeked from behind him, saw nothing. Izrak hissed a warning and pulled her back as he pressed their bodies against the wall. A minute passed, and he looked again. He told her to run and took off. Elishei did not look back until they were well beyond the city. She wondered what Izrak had seen, what could cause him such fear, and was about to ask. But she thought better of it.

The girl did not really want to know.

Dusk passed, and the sleepy eye of a gibbous moon was waking over the eastern hills as the earth-steppers came to the old church of the Redeemer. There they would rest for the night.

Izrak led the girl to the room in which he had found her the day prior. The room was dark but for the moonlight, tinted by the stained-glass hues of red, blue, and green as Elishei lay wrapped in her cloak upon the decaying rug. Izrak sat in the shadows, back against the wall opposite the door, his sword lying across his knees.

Though she was tired, a nagging question kept Elishei awake. With a sigh, the girl rolled over to face him.

"When we met, where were you going?"

"I was traveling to Sevast, looking… for an old friend."

"Is he like you?"

"Yes."

"I've been to Sevast, once, when I was a little girl. My papa had to go to find work on the fishing ships. After my mom died… He said the pay was better than anything in Ryaz. Since there wasn't anyone else to take care of Grigor and me, he brought us with him. We got to stay with his friend, Fanas, and his wife, for a few moons while he was gone. Zarai was good to us… I miss her."

"What happened to your father?"

"… Some thief killed him. A few days after we returned home."

"I am sorry, Elishei…"

"Why did you chase after me? Was it because of your daughter?"

"… You are so much like Cila. More than you can ever know… I saw her in you. So I pursued you, hoping that I might be able to save a life instead of taking one. In so doing, I thought to redeem whatever remains of my soul."

"Did you?"

"No…"

Elishei watched as Izrak traced his fingers over the blade. She swore the runes were glowing faintly, a ghostly blue luminescence that could be mistaken for the moon's light.

"Not yet."

* * *

Novogor had changed during the intervening decades since Izrak had last seen his ancestral home. Walls the height of three tall men, built with massive logs of pine and spruce, fortified the city. The sections of the wall housing the gates and their towers had since been rebuilt with white stone that shone golden in the early evening sun. Cathedrals whose age was passing into antiquity rose above the walls, gold-domed and decadent from neglect. Fanes of strange gods, old and new, now festered among the shadows cast by the once great churches. Magnificent stone palaces sprawled atop hillocks among a lattice of wide avenues that descended to the muddied, rutted streets of the merchant's quarter; from which, an endless flow of carts traveled to the docks at Novogor's southern tip, where low-decked junks with square, battened sails floated down the Algov to unload cargo brought from the Satar Empire in the east.

Yet it was into the city's northern quarter—the oldest part of Novogor—where Elishei led Izrak.

Past crumbling structures choked by the ramshackle hovels of the peasants who existed there, the warrior and his charge moved through narrow streets and twisted alleys, accompanied by the clatter of shutters, the slamming of doors, and the whispers of the curious few who had grown accustomed to the sight of death's passage. Izrak took the lead, for Elishei's destination was now clear. And as evening sank into twilight, the brace of wanderers approached the ancient Tower of Rognai.

Izrak and Elishei took shelter in the shadows of an abandoned hut that offered a clear view of the stronghold. Built by the warriors of the Redeemer's Crusade, Rognai had witnessed the passage of nearly five centuries. Drawing on the western influences of its architects, the stronghold was a pariah among others of its kind in Enostran. At fifty feet, octagonal in shape, the Tower of Rognai had once been a symbol of might in a land besieged by the evil of the Great Serpent. Cyclopean stone blocks formed walls rising thirty feet, lined with crenellated parapets. Rognai's main gate, flanked by machicolated towers standing thirty-five feet tall, was closed off by thick, iron-banded oak doors. A trio of men armed with spears and short swords stood before the gate. Izrak spotted a pair of archers atop each tower.

We cannot go that way. Too dangerous," Izrak said. "If I were alone…"

Elishei lowered the hood of her cloak. "They brought us in another way. A small gate on the other side of the wall, closer to the tower. I only saw one man guarding it from the inside. And there's a hidden passage near the gate that goes into the dungeons. Gromm showed me. That's how I escaped."

"I know of no such gate."

"Maybe they built it recently?"

To smuggle Orved's prisoners in secret...
"Lead on, child."

Elishei smiled, nodded, and they slipped
out of the hut into the gloaming.

* * *

Cautious, Izrak stepped to the edge of
the small grove screening the postern gate.
He pointed at the gate. Elishei nodded as she
crouched beside him. The gate itself was little
more than a large wooden door, but there
was neither a handle nor any apparent way of
gaining access from the outside.

"How are we going to get in?" Elishei
whispered. "Can you force it open somehow?"

"Not without alerting anyone nearby,"
Izrak said as he handed his satchel to the girl.
"Wait here. Do not move until I call you to
me."

"Where are you going?" Elishei hissed
through her teeth as the warrior dashed to the
wall beside the postern.

Reaching it, Izrak removed his gloves,
tucked them inside his belt. After studying
the wall for a moment, he lifted his hand and
ran his bare fingers over the stone until the

tips snagged. Such a wall would be unscalable by mortal hands. Yet the dead may take paths forbidden to the living. With the grace of a spider crawling on its web, Izrak climbed the wall in mere seconds. Raising his head slowly over the parapet, he looked for any patrols. Spying none, the warrior swung his legs over the side, landing in a crouch upon the wall walk.

Izrak peered over the edge toward the gate. *Just as she said.* Only one man stood guard on the door, facing away. A ghost upon the wall, the warrior clung to the shadows cast by neighboring buildings as he climbed down part way, then dropped silently to the ground below.

The instant he landed, Izrak darted towards the guard, closing his fingers as a vise around the man's neck. Breath squealed from the man as Izrak's hands tightened. A sharp crack silenced the guard, and his body went limp. As he lowered the body, Izrak heard the rustling of brush and the tread of boots approaching from behind.

"Oy, Pavil! Careful where you step over there." The newcomer laughed. "I left a big— What the hell!" the guard cried as he drew his short sword and charged.

Unsheathing his sword as he spun about, Izrak parried the guard's overhead strike. In a single motion, Izrak thrust, sending Cila's blade through the man's throat. Blood spurted from his mouth as he pawed at his neck. Izrak withdrew his blade, and the man crumpled.

The warrior waited, listened. No one else appeared.

Izrak approached the gate, drew back the bolt, and pushed it open. He beckoned to Elishei. "Quickly, child."

"How did you—" the girl started to say as she ran over.

"Quiet," Izrak said, taking her by the shoulder, guiding her through the portal. "Move. Do not look down." Elishei blanched when she saw the blood on his sword, but did as she was told.

"Where is this passage you spoke of?" Izrak asked when they were past the gate.

Elishei rushed by him, pointing to where the second guard had emerged. "Over there. Behind those bushes… What's that smell?"

"Watch your step," Izrak said, following close by. As they moved through the brush into a small clearing, he suddenly tugged Elishei to the side. Before she could say anything, he asked, "Where is it?"

She glanced back over her shoulder, then: "There. Under that grate. Stairs go down to a tunnel that'll take us to the dungeons."

"I see it." Izrak tried to lift the grate. The crosshatch of iron bars groaned but did not yield. "Locked…"

Elishei bit her lip, brushed the hair out of her eyes. "One of those guards probably had the key."

"I told you not to look."

"I didn't. I'm not scared. I'll go and check." She started to turn, but Izrak placed a hand on her shoulder, held her in place.

"No need." The warrior faced the grate, taking his sword in both hands. He lifted the blade to his forehead, uttering an archaic prayer. The runes on Cila's blade flashed with azure fire, and Izrak smote the grate. Cila cleaved through the iron bars as a scythe through wheat. The sundered grate fell to the landing with muffled clangor.

"Stay behind me," Izrak said as he stepped onto the stairs, Elishei at his back, and with Cila raised before him, they descended into the dungeons of Rognai.

XII

FERRYMAN

All that awaited Izrak and Elishei at the bottom of the stair was the stench of death and human waste. A portal opened upon the dimly lit landing, which they passed through into a large sluice chamber. Extending several yards before them, the chamber was lined with rough stone pillars supporting a vaulted ceiling just visible in the dim light of the torches below. Shallow gutters filled with sewage emptied through narrow drains set into the walls.

Standing among the shadows at the far end was a large iron door, a faint light emanating from beyond the threshold.

"Through there?" Izrak asked as they stepped further into the chamber.

Elishei simply nodded, her face pinched from the malodor.

As they approached, the chamber echoed with laughter and the screech of rusted hinges; Izrak seized Elishei, pulled her with him into the cover of an adjacent pillar as the door swung open. Two swarthy men entered, cudgels and daggers hanging from their belts.

"I'll give him that! He got a good shot at you. Don't deny it!" the lead man said, laughter dying on his lips.

The second man spat, rubbed his jaw, said, "Lucky's what it was... I'd gut the little bastard myself, but the master will do far worse."

"True, that," the leader said as they turned, headed towards a side passage. "Maybe he's not so lucky after all." His laughter drifted back from inside the passage.

"Too bad the rat's sister isn't here to hear his screams..." the second said, following. Elishei gasped, but Izrak held her, covering her mouth as she struggled to run off. The second spoke again: "Speaking of rats—where is Gromm, anyways?"

"How the hell should I know? On an errand for the master, I expect. He probably..."

The rest faded away with their footsteps into silence. "No, no!" Elishei groaned as she broke from Izrak's hold and rushed towards the door.

"Wait, child," Izrak said, chasing after her into the next chamber.

Wide eyes peered out from gaunt, grime-covered faces, over tiny hands gripping the bars of the cells of a vast, circular dungeon. Some whimpered, faint cries escaping their cracked lips. Others reached grasping hands at Elishei as she flitted between the cells. Most of the captive children remained silent. Checking the last cell, Elishei turned to Izrak, her breathing coming in short bursts.

"He's not here... Grigor!"

"Quiet," Izrak hissed, clutching the girl's shoulders to calm her.

"Let go!" She shrugged off his hands, faced away, and moved deeper into the chamber.

"Elishei, you must—"

A pair of giant hands, gnarled and sickly, seized Izrak by the shoulders. Then, he was hurtling through the air and plummeted to the floor. The warrior rolled to a crouch, his sword held out before him. *What is this new horror?*

Looming over the center of the chamber, rising a head and a half taller than Izrak, a malformed giant stood on mismatched legs, one longer than the other and thick as the trunk of an oak; his barrel chest heaved with each labored breath beneath a coarse tunic stretched too thin. His massive, corded arms quivered with ogreish strength; his small, furious eyes glittered darkly under a sloping brow.

"Do not touch her." The giant's voice was an earthquake.

Elishei whirled about. Realization smacked her face. "Izrak, wait—"

Too late. The ogre's charge was a rockslide. Izrak could do nothing but roll out of his path. As the warrior rose, he slashed at the oversized leg. Cila's edge bit deep. The ogre roared, swung at Izrak, his great fist slamming into the warrior's chest like a battering ram. Izrak crashed into the wall and slumped to the floor in a daze. The impact wrenched Cila from his grip, the sword clattering to the ground beside him.

Thunderous steps: Izrak looked up, shifted his head to the side as the ogre's fist hammered the wall, pulverizing the stone blocks. The ogre lifted his fists overhead, roaring as he brought them down. Izrak evaded obliteration, rolled towards Cila, lifting the blade as he leapt to his feet. The warrior had barely recovered when the ogre swung again. Ducking the strike, Izrak shot forward, slashing at the ogre's smaller leg. Bellowing in pain, the monster dropped to his knee; unable to support the weight, he fell to his hands.

Sword in hand, using the crossguard, Izrak drove his fist with bone-crushing force into the ogre's head. Blood streamed from his mouth; he roared, struggling to rise. Again, Izrak struck with an iron fist. The ogre lurched forward onto his hands, head lowered, and his neck exposed.

Azure flames ignited in his eyes as Izrak lifted his sword overhead. He swung—the blade stopped, edge ringing, a hairsbreadth from Elishei as she clung to the ogre's side, shielding him.

"Izrak, don't!" she cried.

The ogre blinked and shook his head, gaped at Elishei kneeling beside him.

"Gromm… I'm sorry. This warrior, Izrak, is helping me. He came here to free my brother and the others. And you, too." Elishei peered back at Izrak, lips tight, eyes narrowed.

Izrak nodded, sheathed his sword. "Forgive me, Gromm." He moved to Gromm's other side. "Let me help you." Together, Izrak and Elishei helped the giant to his feet. Izrak tore strips from Elishei's cloak and quickly bandaged the wounds on his legs.

"Thank... you..." Gromm said as he steadied himself against the wall. "Sorry."

"It's all right, Gromm," Elishei said softly. "Please, where is Grigor? What happened to him?"

A dozen children now stood at their cell doors, the staccato of their excited whispers puncturing the silence of the chamber.

"Grigor... with the master... In the ritual chamber."

"Where, Gromm?"

The giant gestured to a set of iron doors at the other end of the dungeon.

"Can you walk?"

Gromm nodded.

"Free the children," Izrak said, looking at Elishei, "take them, guide them out the way we came. Wait for me in the grove beyond the wall. Gromm will keep you safe."

Elishei grabbed his arm as Izrak stepped towards the doors, her eyes glistening with tears.

Izrak held her cheek. "These children need you. Your strength will give them courage. I promise you, Elishei, I will bring your brother back to you."

The girl wiped her eyes and smiled.

Gromm waited with the children clinging to him near the dungeon entrance. Elishei glanced one last time at the warrior, then joined the others as they fled.

Izrak faced the entrance to the ritual chamber. *And I will drag Orved's black soul screaming across the River.*

* * *

Izrak Laav stepped into a long antechamber, bereft of light but for the putrid green luminescence seeping from the man-sized vats lining the walls at even intervals. Caution guided his steps as he proceeded further. A tangled mass of cables and tubes, like the choking roots of the Dead Woods, splayed out from the bases of the vats, connecting to various apparatus of alien and sinister design. *What evil lives in this place?*

Eldritch tomes and alchemical implements infested the walls. Meat hooks hung from chains in the ceiling that clinked softly with a rhythmic sway, generated by the vibrations of an almost imperceptible flow of blasphemous energies.

A black iron door, illuminated by the dim glow of violet flames burning in lamps mounted on either side, stood closed at the end of the chamber. The vats near the entrance had been empty except for the vile fluids contained within. Yet, as Izrak neared the door, he saw that the vats, here, were anything but.

What sickness has festered beneath our feet? Inside each vat were the mutilated, deformed bodies of children in various stages of transformation. None of the—experiments— appeared to have been successful. The children showed no signs of life.

Izrak wished that he could feel the shock, the despair, the cosmic sorrow born of such horrifying affliction, that it could only be remedied by a single, final plunge into the Void—into the depths of eternal madness. But the only thing Izrak Laav felt was wrath; the blood that no longer flowed through his veins boiled; the heart that no longer beat hammered against his chest; the tattered remains of a soul, clinging to the last vestiges of humanity, burned with a heat that could no longer be contained.

Izrak's roar exploded from within, his eyes erupting with the cerulean flames of judgement, the runes of Cila's blade ablaze with the light of holy retribution; the warrior's battle

cry was a thunderous horn blast, heralding the
end of days, and the coming of Orved Sepah's
final doom.

Turning to the door, Izrak lifted his sword
and struck. The blade sheared through the
metal, the force of the strike blasting the door
apart into molten halves. Izrak surged into the
ritual chamber.

At the center of the octagonal chamber
was an altar of gleaming obsidian. A pentacle
engraved around the altar's base emanated a
hellish glow. Lying upon the altar was a young
man of seventeen summers, black haired,
covered in a dark ritual garb that clung to a
body coated with sweat and delirium. *Grigor*!

Grigor's deep amber eyes rolled over, fixed
on Izrak.

Standing over him was a man clothed in
black robes trimmed with cloth of gold; a
gold circlet crowned his head, adorning his
brow with a sanguine ruby. His silver hair was
close-cropped and unkempt. At once in the
prime of youth, and yet, in the ancient depths
of age beyond counting, the smooth, pale skin
of his narrow face was framed by low, sharp
cheekbones, set with a long, sloping nose and
thin, pale blue lips.

The sorcerer intoned a chant that was reaching a crescendo, held a dagger above the boy, its tip poised to plunge into Grigor's heart.

"Orved Sepah!" Izrak brandished his sword. "Your end has come."

Orved looked down upon the warrior and sneered. "Has it?"

The warrior lunged. That same instant, the pentacle at the base of the altar flashed crimson; the sorcerer lifted his free hand towards Izrak, making a fist.

Izrak was bound in place, petrified by some unseen force. His body shook with the strain of his futile attempts to free himself.

"Miserable undead wretch!" Orved's laughter skittered across the walls of the chamber. "You dare turn your blade against me, your master?" His laughter ceased. The sorcerer tilted his head. "Yet you grave-spawn are a rebellious kind. Effective, to be sure, but unruly. No matter. Your time will soon be at an end... Ah, yes, the Ferryman himself. Izrak Laav. Should you not be fetching the soul of the Black Bear? Still, you are here... Did Elishei bring you to me?"

Grigor groaned at the mention of his sister's name, writhing atop the altar. Orved slapped him into silence. Izrak raged against his invisible chains.

"It must be. Then my wolves have failed me... Did you slay them, Ferryman?"

Izrak's deathly glare was his only reply.

Orved scowled, pressed long fingers to his lips. "I see. Disappointing. I raised them from pups, yes. And they displayed such promise. More so than Gromm, certainly. All he managed to do was—survive. Took me hundreds of trials, hundreds of sacrifices... My demons are so greedy with their knowledge. They simply will not accept the souls of adults. Still, it works to our benefit. The children are far more—malleable."

"Silence, you heretic fiend!" Izrak's fury drove him. He managed a quaking step forward. "You sell the souls of those the Redeemer has charged you to protect. And for what?"

"Power, of course. The Light has long since abandoned us. What good is faith in an absent god? Who is there to hear our prayers? Who is there to protect us in time of utmost need?" Malice split the sorcerer's face with a wicked grin. "The Redeemer? No... The Dragon. Ah, yes, *he* listens! He grants his favor willingly, real power... to those who are willing to pay the price."

Orved flicked his blade across the palm of
his hand, lifted it overhead. Blood rilled down
his arm. The sorcerer uttered a spell; the lines
of the pentacle flared, and cords of dark energy
burst from the ground, coiling around his arm.
Orved aimed his hand at Izrak, and tendrils
of blood and shadow shot from his fingers to
strangle the warrior's limbs and neck.

Izrak felt his strength waning, as if the
sorcery binding his soul to his body was being
undone. Orved was siphoning the necromantic
power that animated the withering undead.

The warrior fell to his knees. Cila grew
heavy in his hand. His vision faded.

The words came to him on motes of light
from the dark. Izrak uttered the prayer his
mother had taught him as a child. *She said this
prayer would always protect me. Four centuries
have failed to prove her false…*

Cila's runes flared as Izrak lifted the sword
and began to rise.

Blood flowed freely from Orved's hand.
Shaking from strain and anger, the sorcerer
dropped the dagger, redoubled his efforts to
subdue Izrak.

Behind the sorcerer, Grigor stirred at the
clangor of the steel upon stone. The boy looked

down, staring at the dagger, his eyes glazed in stupor. His gaze drifted to the sorcerer, followed the lashes of his spell to the dead man, watching listlessly as Izrak once more began to fade.

Then the boy's eyes cleared, shooting back to the dagger. Grigor seized the blade and plunged it into the sorcerer's back.

Izrak felt his strength surge back into him as Orved howled in pain. The sorcerous tongues enveloping him loosened. The warrior shot to his feet and, with a flash of Cila's blade, severed the tendrils of Orved's spell.

The force of Orved's dark sorcery rebounded, transfiguring his wounded hand to red crystal that then crawled along his forearm, cracked, splintered, and shattered. The sorcerer cried in agony, clutching the jagged stump.

Seeing his chance, Izrak charged the sorcerer. He thrust at Orved's heart.

Orved lifted his remaining hand, and Izrak's blade was turned aside by the sorcerer's barrier. Dark energy crackled with arcs of pale green light.

Izrak lifted Cila overhead; the runes blazed, and the blade flashed a brilliant white. He brought down his sword and shattered the barrier.

Orved fell back against the altar, pleading for his life.

The warrior approached Orved, silent as death's whisper. The sorcerer screamed as Izrak lifted him bodily by the throat and drove Cila's blade through his black heart. Orved's screams died on the edge of the sword; his body withered, turning to dust in Izrak's hand.

* * *

Izrak Laav stood upon the porch of the old church, watching the children play with Gromm in the light-dappled shade of the willow. Color had returned to the bark, and young leaves were budding on the branches swaying in the morning breeze. Beauty yet remained in the world. *Peace is still possible.*

Izrak felt a happiness he had not experienced for years unremembered. At last, he had something to smile about. Izrak chuckled quietly to himself as Grigor emerged from the church.

"Elishei is feeling better," Grigor said as he stood beside the warrior. "She's asleep now."

"Good. She can finally rest, knowing that you and the others are safe." Izrak looked at the boy—*the young man*—still amazed at his resemblance to Ryol. *Even his bravery, his fighting spirit, is every bit the son that I remember…*

Grigor faced the doors, ran his hand over the burning swords engraved upon them. "Thank you. For saving my sister, for looking out for her." He glanced back, cheeks flushed and smiling. "And thanks… for coming back for me."

Izrak turned to him. "I am leaving tomorrow. It will be for you now to protect your family."

The young man breathed deep, released it.

"Are you ready?"

"I am."

"Come with me."

Izrak led him to the side room. Inside, he gave Grigor a short sword scavenged from one of Orved's brigands. Izrak spent the next several hours training him in the basics of swordplay. Grigor learned quickly. Somehow, Izrak had known that he would.

Later, Izrak sat beneath the willow, while the others ate their evening meal, watching as the sun took root in the hills, and twilight bloomed in the west. Elishei appeared, sitting beside him without a word. After a moment, she leaned over, resting her head upon his shoulder. They remained that way for a time. For how long, Izrak Laav cared not...

Izrak spoke first: "Have you decided?"

Smiling, the girl nodded. "We're going to stay."

The warrior was silent.

"Where will you go?"

"Sevast."

"To find your friend?"

"No." Izrak closed his fingers around Cila's hilt. "I expect he will find me."

Epilogue

Gray waves lapped against the wharf as a dog licks its chops in anticipation of a long-awaited meal. Grave clouds of steel closed in, laid siege to the moon, cutting off its waning light; mounting winds stirred the Tyomnimor, the roiling waters of the Dark Sea heralding the storm massing in the east. Izrak Laav stood upon the wharf, black cloak billowing, a flickering shade against that sea of darkness.

On his palm rested the Coin of Akheron. Never, it seemed to him, had one weighed so heavily. For every decision has a price. *And the price is paid.* Izrak threw the coin into the harbor, the sound of its passing lost among the churning shadows below.

"You are, and have always been, a sentimental fool, Ferryman…"

The warrior turned to face him—at last.

A bear's skull mounted on his right

shoulder, joined to a cloak of black bear hide
rippling over a mail coat of black steel, Zheso
Strakh stood atop the embankment, embers of
bloodstone witch-fire smoldering in his eyeless
pits above his wicked grin of jagged teeth.

The barbarian undead leapt from the
embankment, landing in a crouch. Zheso rose
to stand a head taller than Izrak. The pilings
of the wharf shook beneath his tread as he
approached, lifting the battleaxe from his back.

"And you have not lost your fondness for
drama, Black Bear." Cerulean fire kindled in his
eyes as Izrak drew Cila.

Zheso halted, lifted his chin. "Pretty
sword." He brandished his axe. "Though I
wonder if she has any bite." Not looking away
from Izrak, the barbarian reached into a pouch
on his belt, said, "You made quite a mess back
in Novogor, Izrak Laav," as he withdrew a Coin
and tossed it onto the planks between them. "I
have been offered a chance at redemption. My
place in the order will be restored. All I must
do… is destroy you."

"Is that all?" Izrak assumed a fighting
stance.

Zheso stepped forward, lifting his axe
overhead. He swung, the head biting deep into
the wood as its edge sundered the coin. Leaving

the axe where it stood, the barbarian came before Izrak. "To Hell with the order."

Cloaks fluttered in the wind. The pilings groaned against the rush of the waves. Izrak grunted, sheathing his sword.

"What will you do?" Zheso asked.

"I am leaving Enostran."

"And your Omen?"

Izrak turned back to the sea. "Olesia is securing our passage to Satar."

"The Empire is poor refuge," Zheso said as he moved beside him. "That land is tainted by sinister gods and foul sorceries."

"Yes. And I see now that Enostran has become no different. Satar's influence is spreading, and I fear the High Priests have been corrupted. Orved was creating soldiers, building an army of demons. His sorcery was of the Dragon. Of that, I am certain. Garyn'zmei survived. The priests have betrayed Enostran, betrayed our home. I know they plot the destruction of The Call, but for what purpose, I am unsure. Yet, I do not intend to wait. I shall seek the Dragon's heart in the east," lighting arced across the clouds; the sky shuddered under the roar of thunder, "and tear it out."

Zheso said nothing.

A moment passed, and Izrak said, "Come with us, you and Silisa."

"No." Zheso turned and loosed his axe, slinging its haft over his shoulder. "As you said, this is our home. If you are going off to play the hero, you will need us to deal with the priests." The barbarian moved towards the embankment. "The Dragon's heart is yours, Ferryman." Zheso glanced back at Izrak. "Leave its heads to me… All this talk has made me hungry. It is time for the Black Bear to hunt."

Thus ends the first tale of Izrak the Deathless....

ENJOYED THE STORY?
JOIN OUR NEWLETTER TO STAY INFORMED!

PANDEMONIUM AWAITS.

ASHEN RIDER by James D. Mills releases in
Paperback on December 19th, 2025.

When her mother is claimed by Death a second time,
Kateryna is forced to abandon her afterlife and descend
into Pandemonium—a shattered underworld shaped
by pain, memory, and buried sin. To save her mother's
soul, she must join forces with her estranged father,
whose devotion to a fallen goddess set this all in motion.
Hunted by Morgana, the Goddess Corrupted and her
chosen griffin-riders, Kateryna must journey through the
shadows and confront the reality of her own dark past—
because in Pandemonium, death is only the beginning.

www.ingramcontent.com/pod-product-compliance
Lightning Source LLC
Chambersburg PA
CBHW050402110726
47899CB00008B/2622